Tom had po͏   and
times. Walking   eth,
he remembered how sure he'd been that it
could never happen.

But looking at her, feeling her hand in his, he
knew it was right. After all these weeks, he had
to bare his soul to her. He had to unload everything. *Everything*, he reminded himself. *My life,
my family. Everything.*

He led Elizabeth into his room and kicked
the door shut behind him. The place was a pigsty, but he was too focused to care.

All he could think was, *Tell her. Tell her now.*

Bantam Books in the Sweet Valley University series
Ask your bookseller for the books you have missed

SWEET VALLEY UNIVERSITY™

The Love of Her Life

Written by
Laurie John

Created by
FRANCINE PASCAL

BANTAM BOOKS
NEW YORK · TORONTO · LONDON · SYDNEY · AUCKLAND

RL 6, age 12 and up

THE LOVE OF HER LIFE
A Bantam Book / August 1994

Sweet Valley High® and Sweet Valley University™
are trademarks of Francine Pascal
Conceived by Francine Pascal
Produced by Daniel Weiss Associates, Inc.
33 West 17th Street
New York, NY 10011

ISBN: 0-553-56310-6

Published simultaneously in the United States and Canada

Bantam Books are published by Bantam Books, a division of Bantam
Doubleday Dell Publishing Group, Inc. Its trademark, consisting of the
words "Bantam Books" and the portrayal of a rooster, is Registered in
U.S. Patent and Trademark Office and in other countries. Marca
Registrada. Bantam Books, 1540 Broadway, New York, New York 10036.

PRINTED IN THE UNITED STATES OF AMERICA

OPM   0 9 8 7 6 5 4 3 2 1

To Taryn Rebecca Adler

Chapter One

"Jessica! Jessica!"

Jessica Wakefield's body went rigid with fear on her brother Steven's couch. Hot tears streaked her face.

Loud, crashing sounds echoed down the hallway. It was Mike McAllery, banging on every door, calling Jessica's name. She heard doors opening, a woman's scream, doors slamming shut.

"I'm going to tell him to get lost," Steven said.

"D-don't let him in here," Jessica begged Steven's girlfriend, Billie. "Please, no matter what he says, don't let him in here."

Billie put her arm around Jessica's shoulders. "Nobody's letting him in," she promised. "If he doesn't go away, I'll call the cops."

"Jessica!" Mike cried.

1

It was a wail of intense grieving. Jessica could hardly recognize his voice. She put her hands over her ears.

"Jessica!" The door to the apartment started rattling. "Jessica, you have to let me in!"

"P-please . . . you can't . . ." Jessica was sobbing now. "I'm scared . . ."

The door pounded violently.

"No! Go away!" Jessica shrieked.

Steven started toward the door. "That's it!" he shouted. "It's time he got a chance to pick on somebody his own size."

Jessica's nails dug into Billie's knee. "No!" she screamed. "No, don't open the door! You don't understand—"

Billie was on her feet, too, heading for the telephone. "Steven! Steven, don't! I'm calling the police."

Steven kept walking as though he hadn't heard them. "I'm not afraid of that punk. You hear me, you cheap hood?" he shouted, his hand on the doorknob. "I'm not afraid of you. You want to fight, then you've got someone to fight. Let's see if you'll push me around the way you push around my sister."

"Steven, don't!" both Billie and Jessica screamed at the same moment.

Jessica jumped up from the couch, her heart pounding wildly.

2

"Please! He's got a—"

But it was too late.

The door swung open and Mike McAllery stumbled into the room, a snub-nosed revolver in his hand. The muzzle aimed right at Steven's chest.

When Billie saw the flash of metal in his hand, she screamed.

"I want my wife!" Mike shouted. "Get out of my way, Wakefield. I want my wife."

"You can't have her!" Steven shouted back.

As if in slow motion, Steven snatched the gun. He tore it from Mike's grip and it skidded across the floor. Both men dove for it.

"Oh, God, no!" Jessica screamed, backing up against the wall. "Stop them!"

Billie leapt for the phone.

Both men were tangled on the floor, struggling closer and closer toward the gun.

Billie was already dialing 911 when the shot rang out. Both men collapsed and lay lifeless on the floor. A blue cloud of smoke hovered over them. Everything went totally silent for a second that seemed to last for hours.

And then another scream tore apart the night.

"Why don't I get us another drink?" William White whispered, pulling gently away from

3

Elizabeth Wakefield. "All this passionate kissing is making me thirsty."

Elizabeth didn't so much answer as breathe a yes. All of this passionate kissing was making her nervous. How had it started? What was she doing in William's apartment? She watched him disappear into the kitchen and sat up, straightening her clothes. She had to get out of here, that was definite. When he came back with the drinks, she'd tell him that she'd had a wonderful evening but that she really had to go.

She stood up. "Where's the bathroom?" she called.

William stood in the doorway in his black tuxedo. He'd taken off his bow tie and unbuttoned the top two buttons of his shirt.

"Through the bedroom, Elizabeth." He flashed a loaded smile. The light winked seductively in his eyes. "You can't miss it."

He was right; she couldn't miss it. It was one of those cavernous old bathrooms with a giant tub with clawed lion's feet. Elizabeth washed her face and combed through her long, tangled golden hair with her fingers. She was wearing a sleeveless black evening gown and pumps. One strap hung off her shoulder. The string of pearls that she'd borrowed from her friend Nina Harper to wear to the charity ball were wrapped around her neck like a collar.

4

She stared into her sea-green eyes in the mirror and cocked her eyebrows in disbelief. Tonight William had been so attentive and sweet that she'd almost forgotten how uneasy he usually made her. She'd especially forgotten this when William suggested they go up to his place for a nightcap after the ball. But that uneasy feeling was definitely returning.

And by tomorrow morning, this will all have been a bad dream. As if it never happened . . .

On her way back into the living room she stopped to look through the books on William's shelves. Auden, Austen, Byron, Cervantes, Chekhov, Dostoyevsky, Eliot, Gogol . . . It was like a library. The room seemed as mysterious as William did: dark wood paneling, plush blood-red carpeting, a black leather couch lined with red satin pillows. Elizabeth ran her fingers across the spines of William's books. She loved their musty smell.

Then, as if by itself, her finger stopped on one. Between Stein and Stendhal was a leather-bound book with no inscription.

Almost feeling as though the book were pulling her hand toward it, Elizabeth reached out and took it from the shelf. It looked very old and valuable, so she opened it carefully.

Inside, the pages were yellow and crisp, but the writing was indecipherable. The letters of all the words seemed to be switched around.

"How weird," she whispered. "It's written in code." From the way the entries fit together, it looked as though it might be a log of some kind. Her heart was starting to pound as she flipped through the pages. Suddenly her eye was drawn to one of the few things not in code. It was a name: Bryan Nelson, followed by a date. November thirteenth, the night of the attack! Elizabeth's mind was racing.

"What are you doing, Elizabeth? Don't tell me you got lost."

She looked up, startled. William was standing in the doorway, his eyes on the book in her hand.

"I'm sorry," she said quickly, snapping it shut. "I was just looking to see what you had." She went to push the strange book back in place, but as she did, something that had been wedged between the pages fluttered toward the floor.

They both watched it drift slowly down like a feather.

It wasn't until it landed that Elizabeth could see what it was: a silver bookmark.

Her eyes narrowed. She could practically hear her heart stop beating. Engraved into the top of the bookmark was the sign of the broken star.

"Steven!" Billie screamed, huddling over both bodies. She rolled Steven over. The front of his shirt was drenched in blood. "Oh, God!"

Jessica held her head in her hands. "No, no, no!" she cried over and over. Her head was pounding with one thought: *Mike killed my brother.*

Slowly, miraculously, Steven's eyes opened and he sat up. He looked down at himself. His eyes were wide with terror. His hands gleamed crimson with blood as he raised them to his face.

"Oh no," he muttered. He turned and looked at Mike. Mike's eyes were closed, his face already as white as a sheet.

"Mike?" Steven said. He took hold of his shoulders. "Mike? Mike?"

Mike didn't move. He lay as still as a stone. He wasn't breathing.

Billie sprinted back to the phone.

Jessica crouched in the corner of the room. Her entire body shook convulsively. *Steven isn't dead.* Her mind grasped at the knowledge. Her eyes moved to Mike, and she stared in disbelief. Her first love, *her husband,* once so full of energy and rebellion, was now lying motionless on the floor as his life spilled out of him in a spreading red pool.

William's face hardened for less than a second before he recovered his composure and grinned in his arrogant, it's-my-world way. He reached for the light switch and plunged the room into darkness. Elizabeth felt his breath on her face.

"Now why go snooping through other people's shelves?" he said in a silky smooth voice. "It's so unlike you." She felt his hand on her waist. "But in case you're curious, I'll explain. I'm the Honor Society secretary. Those pages are the society's minutes, which are, by the way, confidential."

Elizabeth felt herself taken by the arms. She froze with fear.

For months she'd been obsessed by an organization known around campus as the secret society. At first she'd heard only bits and pieces, mostly rumors about a mysterious group of supremacists who wielded control not only at Sweet Valley University and other campuses but in places of power all over the country. They'd seemed so remote to her as to be unreal, more rumor than anything else. Until the racial attack on her friends Nina Harper and Bryan Nelson a few weeks ago. After that Elizabeth hadn't been able to think of anything but tracking down the leader of that gang of thugs and bringing him to justice. Tom Watts, her investigative-reporting partner for the campus TV station, WSVU, turned out to know more about it than she'd ever imagined. He had confessed to her that he'd once been a member. He'd even shown her a ring with the society's top-secret symbol: the broken star.

Now, in William's arms, Elizabeth felt her spine go numb. Her knees weakened. Her hands began to shake. She groped along the wall for the light switch and found it. The room seemed to explode with light as the realization swept over her like a wave of ice water.

The man she'd been looking for had been terrifyingly close all along. William White. Her stomach turned at the thought of having kissed him.

She pushed William away, her breath coming in shallow gasps. "Oh, God. It's you!"

Tom huddled in the shadows outside William White's apartment building off-campus. He had been there for two hours now, waiting for Elizabeth. He'd first gone to find her at the charity ball, but Bryan had told him she'd left with William. Tom had gone to Elizabeth's room just in case, hoping against hope that she would be there. But Elizabeth's roommate, Celine Boudreaux, only confirmed Tom's fear.

His brain almost hurt, he'd been thinking so hard. Keeping watch, he'd had nothing to do *but* think, and think hard. He looked up at the apartment house, a massive stone building with turrets and towers and freakish, toothy gargoyles hanging off the roof. In the moonlight it looked like a haunted mansion.

Just the sort of place where the ringleader of the secret society might live, Tom thought.

He had just figured it out that night. He'd been lying on his bed in the dark, trying to pinpoint the exact moment when things began to change between him and Elizabeth.

Until recently they'd had a great working relationship. They'd pried open the lid on an important case involving preferential treatment for star recruits in SVU's athletic department. And they'd begun work on an exposé on the secret society. Everything was going smoothly. Almost too smoothly. Tom's feelings for Elizabeth grew beyond a professional partnership. They grew beyond anything he'd felt for anyone in his life. And he had thought, he had hoped, that he detected hints of feeling from Elizabeth.

And then everything changed. Almost overnight, Elizabeth grew distant, even cold. He could tell she'd stopped trusting him.

He'd racked his brain for something he did or said and found nothing. And then he realized Elizabeth's change of heart occurred around the same time William came on the scene. The impeccably dressed, silk-tongued William White.

10

The wealthy William White. The mysterious and secretive William White.

A couple of days ago, when Tom had shown Elizabeth his ring with the broken star and confessed his involvement with the secret society, she hadn't looked surprised. In fact, she looked convinced. Convinced that *he* was the leader of the secret society, that he was responsible for the society's hatred and violence. She actually seemed *afraid* of him. The thought made his heart ache.

But someone had planted the seeds of that possibility in Elizabeth's mind. Someone had told her not to trust him.

Tom knew beyond a doubt it was William White. The same man who had been unexpectedly busy at a mysterious meeting the other night. The same man whose big-time business connections would be just the fuel a national organization like the secret society would need.

Tom knew William would do anything to deflect Elizabeth's suspicion onto somebody else.

Tom felt his hands clench into fists.

He sure hadn't helped his own case. When he sensed Elizabeth's doubts, he hadn't opened up to her and comforted her, and told her how much he loved her. He'd clammed up. He'd pushed her away. He'd acted wounded and made himself more of a mystery than William.

11

That was just the opening William needed. He'd gotten his foot in the door of Elizabeth's mind and starting prying away. And it had worked. William had won and Tom had lost.

Tom grimaced. Why had he pushed her away? Why hadn't he just told her the truth? He'd been like that for too long: just when he felt himself opening up to someone, he shut himself off.

The light went out in William's apartment. Tom felt his heart crack as if it were made of glass. He could have kicked himself for being such a coward. He should have told Elizabeth everything. They might have had a chance then. But now she was making the huge mistake of falling for William White.

"Watts, you idiot," Tom said out loud.

He had not only succeeded in driving Elizabeth away, he'd set her in the fast lane heading straight for danger.

The light stayed off. Defeated, Tom stepped out of the shadows and started walking home.

Suddenly, in the corner of his eye, he caught a flash of light. William's light was back on. And then, straining to hear through the silence, Tom made out the sound of raised voices. Seconds later the door to the building burst open and Elizabeth came rushing out. Her eyes found him in the darkness, and she threw herself into his arms.

"Oh, my God," Elizabeth cried, burying her face in his shoulder. "It's William!"

Celine lit one cigarette with the smoldering butt of another. Billows of smoke drifted across her bed like clouds on a windy day. She propped herself up on her satin pillows, still wrapped in her purple-magnolia-colored gown. Her face felt bruised. Whenever she spent the evening with Peter Wilbourne, her face hurt for hours afterward.

It was a result of making out with him, which she did more out of boredom than anything like passion. And he wasn't *bad*-looking. As usual, though, her face felt as though she'd spent all night scrubbing it with sandpaper.

She touched her face, but she was no longer thinking of Peter. She was thinking instead of Tom Watts. Tonight was *supposed* to be the night she was finally going to wrap him in a knot around her finger.

It was only recently that Tom had started showing interest in her. Celine wasn't sure why—after all, up to now he'd been so obviously gaga over Little Miss Goody Two-Shoes Wakefield. At first she was suspicious. But then she had thought, *Why look a gift horse in the mouth? You take what you can get in this world.* They'd been out on a couple of dates, but every time Celine thought Tom was going to kiss her, he'd had to make a phone call or run to the bathroom or something. No man had ever resisted kissing her before. But that was part of what she liked about Tom: his charming coyness. It was the hard ones who were the most worth catching.

But then tonight, at the very last minute, Mr. Watts called to say he was sick with a cold and couldn't take her to the ball. A white-hot rush of jealousy had flooded her eyes. She knew this had something to do with Elizabeth. "Never mind feeling sick!" she'd screamed at him over the phone. "You're just not man enough to be seen in public with me!"

The worst part was that she hadn't simply dressed up for him. Celine had made herself drop-dead gorgeous. She'd paid a fortune to a hair salon to torture her honey-blond hair into an alluring pile on top of her head, complete with carefully created escaping curls. She'd spent an entire afternoon trying on gowns, deciding on a complicated combination of ivory taffeta and silk georgette that accentuated her curves but also suggested the flowery innocence of the genteel South. And for what? Nothing, that's what. Celine groaned again and laid her head on the cool pillows.

And just an hour or so ago Tom had barged

his way in here demanding to know where Little Miss America Wakefield was. He looked as strong and gorgeous as ever. He'd obviously made a quick recovery from that cold of his.

Purring like a Cheshire cat, she had told Tom for his own good that Elizabeth had gone home with William. She'd felt a pang of joy when his face dropped. She so enjoyed bursting the bubbles of these stupid Californians, especially of one who had just stood her up. No Southern gentleman would have turned Celine down for the ball, not even if he was suffering from recurrent malaria.

Well, anyway, thank God for Peter Wilbourne, she thought. He was about as interesting as a tree, but at least he made a visibly acceptable substitute. Like an Afghan dog, he looked pretty, but he probably couldn't find his way home from his own driveway.

"Silly boys," Celine drawled, exhaling through a slow smile. She reached for another cigarette, but the pack was empty. As she angrily aimed the wrapper across the room at Elizabeth's tidy, un-slept-in bed, there was a loud knock on the door. Before Celine could reply, the door burst open.

"Why, hello there, sugar," she said, her face lighting up. It was the man of her dreams. The only one whose mind matched her own for cunning and deception.

"Where is she?" William asked evenly. His

hands were thrust deep in a trench coat. His voice was calm and efficient, his pale blue eyes as cold as ice. But right now William's coolness was a front—to Celine he seemed almost manic. The possibility intrigued her.

She plumped up her pillows. "I was just saying to myself how grateful I'd be if some gallant young squire ran on down to the corner store for cigarettes," she said, patting the empty stretch of bed beside her.

William flung his own pack of cigarettes past her, then paced up and down the room. His eyes were jumpy, his movements restless. If Celine hadn't known better, she'd say slick William was actually panicking.

Her pretty face was drawn with concern. "I haven't a clue where Elizabeth is," she said, waving her hand at the empty room. "I thought she was with you. Don't tell me you lost her."

William went to the window. "She'll come back." His hands cemented into white-knuckled fists. Celine came up behind him and slid off his trench coat.

"Shh, relax," she purred, her voice sweeter than syrup. She kneaded his back and turned up the fire under her Southern accent. "You look like you're coming apart at the seams, darling."

She nibbled the back of his neck.

William shrugged Celine off his shoulders.

16

"You're as deep into this as any of us," he hissed.

"What are you talking about?"

He whirled around.

Celine stepped back.

William's mouth curled into a sneer. "She knows."

Todd Wilkins unknotted his tuxedo tie in front of the full-length mirror on his bathroom door. Just a few hours ago, while he was dressing for the ball, he'd actually convinced himself that he still looked like a man with an unlimited future. Despite getting busted for the special treatment given SVU's star athletes, he'd believed that he was still an eligible bachelor any mother would make a fuss over. Now when he looked at himself, all he saw was a tall guy in a wrinkled tux who needed a shave and a haircut. A petty criminal, victim of broken dreams and empty promises.

"I can't believe it's all turned out like this," he murmured to his reflection.

Everyone had treated him like a king when he first arrived at SVU. Most of the other freshmen wouldn't even try to talk to him, as though they were in the presence of royalty. Even the upperclassmen made space at their tables for him whenever he walked into cafeteria.

He could still hear the wild cheers from his

teammates and the applause from his coach at the opening practice of the season, when the first time he got his hands on the basketball he'd hit an outside jumper from thirty feet. All those girls waiting for him to come out of the locker room. *This is what it must be like to be Michael Jordan,* he'd thought back then. Now he felt like Al Capone.

When he had walked into the charity ball, everyone he passed either turned their backs or had a sudden urge for more punch. It was no coincidence that conversation after conversation died just as he came over. The only people who didn't treat him like a leper were the kids Nina and Bryan had brought over from the after-school program—and the kids were only nice to him because they didn't read the papers or watch the news.

"No one at the ball would even talk to me," he reminded his reflection.

Two slim, bronze arms wrapped themselves around him from behind. "I'll talk to you any day," said the silky voice of Lauren Hill.

Todd attempted a smile in the mirror.

"Just wait," she said. "Everyone will see the dean is only making an example of you guys. You'll be cleared, and then they'll all come begging for forgiveness. If there's anything of you left." Lauren traced a wet trail down his neck with her lips, then began nibbling on his collar-bone.

Usually her kisses were as cool and soothing as sweet fruit, but now they were overripe.

Todd shrugged her away and crossed his arms. Lauren considered him in the mirror.

"You're being melodramatic," she snapped, tossing her hair over her shoulders, her personal signal that she was annoyed. "You didn't do anything wrong. You have nothing to worry about."

"Easy for you to say, Lauren," Todd said. "It's not your scholarship on the line. It's not your *career*. If the administration says I took bribes to play basketball for SVU, it doesn't matter whether I did or I didn't. It's what everyone is going to think. And in the outside world it doesn't matter what you do, it matters what everyone *thinks* you do."

Todd was certain that he hadn't done any-thing wrong. Sure, he had gotten preferential treatment from the moment he was accepted to SVU. But no more than any of the other top athletes. None of them had refused, so why should he? It had never occurred to him that there was anything illegal about it. Superathletes brought money and attention to schools, and in exchange they were treated like something spe-cial. That was the silent agreement. It was the way things had always worked—that is, until Elizabeth Wakefield and Tom Watts exposed on the WSVU news the unwritten bargain between the SVU athletic department and its stars.

Lauren nibbled lightly on his ear. "Don't get worked up," she cooed. "Come on, kiss me. I promise it will make you forget your troubles."

"Stop it!" Todd shouted, and swung around. Lauren backed off. Todd squinted at her through his tears. He didn't see a voluptuous redhead. He saw a dark splotch.

"Why can't you understand what this means to me?" he demanded. "You never thought the scandal would amount to anything, but you were wrong. You saw the way people were embarrassed just to be seen with me tonight. And I can't worry about it without you making me feel like a fool. But I'm going to lose my scholarship. I might even be expelled." Todd held out his long arms. "*That's* reality, Lauren. Welcome to the real world."

"And we both know who to thank for it," Lauren muttered. Her lips began to quiver, a sure sign that she was about to cry. "Elizabeth wouldn't have done the story if you were still going out. Maybe you never should have broken up with her."

Lauren had said the same thing the day before, only then it was a tease. "Maybe I shouldn't have," Todd had said, but kissed her back so she'd know he was kidding.

But tonight it sounded like a challenge. And Todd was in no mood to reassure her. He was the one who needed support, but Lauren wasn't there for him when he needed it most. Not the way he wanted.

Not like Elizabeth was. When they were together, he never had to ask Elizabeth for comfort; he never had to ask for anything. She seemed to anticipate his every need.

"Maybe you're right," he murmured. "Maybe I shouldn't have dumped her."

Lauren bolted for the door, tears cascading down her face. Usually when she went home at night, Todd insisted she let him walk her there. This time he just let her go.

"So, how about that kiss you promised me?" Denise Waters said.

"You mean the one *you* promised *me*." Winston Egbert gave himself a quick reality check. His eyes darted around his room: *Yep, there's my desk. Yep, there's my collection of Clint Eastwood posters. Yep, this is my room.* He glanced at his reflection in the mirror. *Yep, there's me. And yep*—this was the part he still had trouble believing—*there's HER. And . . . oh, my God . . . there are my arms—around HER.*

Yesterday he was a campus wimp who not only couldn't get into a fraternity but was almost killed off by one. Earlier today he didn't even have a date to the charity ball. But tonight, tonight he had not only gone to the ball, he had gone with the most beautiful girl at SVU, Denise Waters.

Even though it wasn't even the end of his first semester at college, Winston felt like he had been dreaming about Denise for years. They'd gotten along as well as any couple he knew, but he could never be sure what her feelings were. When she hugged him, she hugged him like a sister. When she kissed him, she kissed him like a friend. But then, earlier that afternoon, she'd come from her room down the hall and invited him to the ball. And now he had the gorgeous object of his desire not only sitting beside him on his bed but wrapped in his arms, right below Clint Eastwood as Dirty Harry.

He closed his eyes and replayed the exact moment at the ball that had changed everything. The sophisticatedly sensual Denise had asked him to teach her how to break-dance. When he'd protested, she'd grabbed his hand and yanked him across the ballroom floor. Suddenly everyone else dancing around them evaporated. It was just the two of them. The music, which up till then had been mostly funk and rap, had instantly switched to something old and slow and soft—Aretha Franklin, Diana Ross, someone like that. He'd felt a strange sensation inside him. It was like someone else had stepped into his body. Someone suave and self-assured, who knew exactly what to do and when to do it. He heard Denise's question all over again: "So it's all right? You'll teach me how?" And he heard his reply, not *his* reply but this other guy's, the one with the perfect lines and impeccable timing and sure hands: "If you let me kiss you, I'll show you anything."

It was magic. The next thing he knew, Denise's arms were around his neck. Her face came close. Her lips . . . All those weeks of throbbing anticipation. Winston had gone into a full body shiver. He almost couldn't stand it. Almost.

Winston opened his eyes. He half-expected Denise to be gone. And when she wasn't, he looked up at Dirty Harry with brotherly understanding: *Know how it feels to be in charge, buddy.*

"What's wrong, Winnie? Why do you keep closing your eyes?"

"Oh, I—I have something in my eye."

A look of protective concern came over Denise's face as she unlatched herself from Winston's waist and began probing his eyes. She peered at each one.

23

"Which?"

"The left."

Winston liked the way Denise looked when she was worried. He imagined that was the way she might look with their children, when they came home from school with scraped knees. Children? *Whoa, there, Win boy,* Winston said to himself. *We're getting a little ahead of ourself, aren't we?*

"I don't see anything," Denise said.

"Try the right."

"I thought you said the left."

"Well, it's the *other* left."

"Come on, Winston," Denise huffed.

Winston laughed. "There's something in both my eyes."

"What does it feel like, an eyelash?"

"It sort of feels like the most beautiful woman in the world, and she's wearing a very sexy ball gown."

Denise squinted at him, pursed her lips in mock annoyance, then poked him in the side. Then the other side. Winston poked back. They brandished their fingers like swords and leapt to their feet. Without a second thought Winston grabbed a pillow and hurled it at her. Denise whipped it back. Laughing and giggling like little kids, they chased each other around the beds, over the beds, knocking over chairs, almost shattering Winston's desk lamp. One by one the buttons at the back of Denise's dress popped. Winston tore a hole in the knee of his pants. Denise swung and missed with a pillow. Winston had a clear shot at her head, and he took it. As the pillow swallowed Denise's face the seams burst and the room rained feathers.

And Winston and Denise, their ball clothes torn, collapsed into bed with their lips pressed together.

Chapter Two

Tom and Elizabeth sat side by side at the sprawling desk in the office of WSVU. Tom leaned over the neat piles of notes Elizabeth had made on the secret society story, moving quickly down page after page with his finger.

Elizabeth still felt the places William White had touched her. They felt bruised. The dark of the office closed around her and Tom, the only light coming from the lamp hovering close over their heads. *Like a protective shroud*, Elizabeth thought. She couldn't help but feel relief just sitting next to Tom. For a fleeting moment she let herself admit that no matter what she said, or wanted to believe, being with Tom Watts was the most comfortable thing in the world.

"Okay," Tom said. "So we both know who we're after now. We both know William White is the leader of the secret society."

"William White," Elizabeth answered. She shivered. "God, what an idiot I am."

But in spite of Elizabeth's revulsion, a sense of relief was creeping in. At last she could start to trust Tom again.

And at last they had the answer to the puzzle that had become an obsession. It wasn't an answer she was prepared for, but still, it was an answer. Now they had the secret society in the crosshairs. Their fingers were on the trigger. Now all they needed was ammunition.

"What evidence do we have?" Tom asked.

"Well, for one thing we have William's log," Elizabeth said. "If we could only get our hands on it. The code didn't look too hard to break." She turned in her chair, excited. "I know! I'll get back into his room. I'll call him and say it was all a misunderstanding. I'll make another date. For dinner, at his place."

She searched Tom's face for his reaction, and when she read what was there, all she could say was, "Bad idea, huh?"

"Bad idea," Tom said.

"Too dangerous?"

"I don't know which of us would feel worse. You going back in there, or me having to wait outside."

A feeling of warmth surged through Elizabeth. *He's protecting me,* she thought.

"Okay," she said. "Plan B. How can we get back in there?"

"We can't get William's log book," Tom said. "We have to get something else."

"What do you mean? I'm sure it's firsthand proof that the society attacked Nina and Bryan. It would probably incriminate them in other unsolved cases, too."

"It won't be there," Tom said grimly. "It's probably locked in a safety deposit box in a bank downtown. They have a procedure if they think they're in danger of being found out."

"You're probably right," Elizabeth said.

"No, Elizabeth. I know I'm right."

For a moment Elizabeth had forgotten. Tom should know about the society's inner workings. He'd been there. She couldn't imagine it. She just couldn't see Tom being a part of all that.

"We have my ring," Tom said.

Elizabeth shook her head. "We need more. That could be anybody's ring. And it doesn't really prove anything."

Tom drummed his fingers on the desk. "What, then?"

Suddenly Elizabeth's eyes brightened. She sat up straight.

"We don't need that log. Or your ring. We have something better. We have *you,* Tom. Your

29

testimony. You'll be the star witness for the prosecution."

Tom winced. "I don't know, Elizabeth. One thing the secret society was very good at was concealing the identities of its members, even from other members. I didn't suspect William was the ringleader much before you did. I don't even know if I can place him at any of the meetings. I don't know if I could identify anybody."

William White, Elizabeth repeated to herself, suddenly distracted. *William White.* How could she have let William White put his hands on her?

"Elizabeth, what's wrong?" Tom asked in alarm. "You're green! Are you sick?"

"No, I'm okay," Elizabeth said. She couldn't help remembering how flattered she had been when William had asked her out. Her first few weeks at college had gone so badly that she'd stopped trusting her heart, her judgment. Somewhere in her mind she had known she shouldn't trust William, but she'd felt confused, and she let his good looks and slick manner impress her. What a fool she had been.

"Although I think I may be sick in the head," Elizabeth said slowly. "And the heart."

Tom looked away. Elizabeth eyed him carefully. *He thinks I'm heartsick,* she thought. *I've learned what William is, and he thinks I'm upset. He thinks I fell in love with William after all.*

"Haven't you ever just wished you could take back something you did?" she said.

"Have I ever," Tom replied quickly.

The way Tom said that made Elizabeth zero in on his face. He seemed to be saying something important, but she didn't know what. He had more nooks and crannies to him than anyone she had ever known before. And what mysteries filled all those little crevices? *You're such a puzzle, Tom Watts. What is this secret cloud that seems to be hanging over you?* she thought.

"William almost had me convinced that *you* were the head of the secret society." Normally Elizabeth would have been embarrassed to say it, but this time she didn't flinch. She looked Tom straight in the eye and waited for his reaction.

He said nothing.

"What's wrong, Tom? We know who we're after now. All we have to do is piece together what we have and lower the net."

Tom wouldn't meet her piercing gaze.

"Come on," Elizabeth pleaded. "There's something wrong. There's something worrying you. You have to tell me."

"Oh, Elizabeth," he whispered, twisting and turning in his chair, looking over his shoulder. "There's so much to tell you. But I can't. Not here. Not now."

*   *   *

31

It just didn't make sense, Jessica thought. The glaring blue lights of the ambulance just didn't agree with this beautiful velvet evening, this infinitely deep sky, this moonlight. The police cruisers kept coming, first one, then three, now seven or eight. It looked like a highway pileup of emergency vehicles. But all Jessica could think about was how this just didn't *look* right.

She heard her name called from far off. It was Billie calling her, but Jessica didn't know where she was. Jessica turned, and there was Billie waving at her, as though from across the parking lot. There were all these police cars, and an ambulance, but all of it seemed so far away. Jessica felt numb all over. She couldn't take anything in. And there was this loud ringing in her head, more like a hum. Then she remembered. The gunshot.

The ringing had started right after the gunshot. She'd seen her brother's lips moving, but she couldn't hear him. She thought she'd gone deaf. But she had read his lips: "I think he's dead, Jess."

Who's dead? she wondered. Then there was Steven, walking out the entrance to the apartment building, followed closely by three or four policemen, into the glow of the emergency lights. His hands were cuffed. He looked like he was in pain. *They really should loosen those hand-*

cuffs, she thought, *because it looks like they're hurting him* . . .

Jessica looked up and saw that every window in the apartment building had a face. People were standing in their robes, with towels wrapped around their shoulders. People just out of the shower. People with aprons on. People were cooking their dinner. *He's dead,* she thought. *Who's dead?*

All at once it came to her. Steven covered with blood, dead. Then not dead. Steven sitting up, turning to the other body. "I think he's dead, Jess," she heard the words in her head. Mike. Mike, her husband. Mike, who'd chased her from the apartment after a terrible fight. Mike, who lay on the kitchen floor, blood pooling around him. Jessica turned and there was Billie, not across the parking lot but right beside her.

"Jessica."

Jessica felt her knees go weak. She leaned into Billie. Billie put both arms around her and held her up.

"I'm sorry," Jessica said. "I don't know what happened. It was like I wasn't there. It was like it wasn't even me."

"Shh, baby," Billie said, rubbing Jessica's back. "I know. I know."

They watched numbly as the three policemen led Steven to a police cruiser and opened the door.

"How did this happen?" Jessica wondered aloud.

The policemen had their hands on Steven's shoulder. They were pushing him into the back-seat. Just before he disappeared, Steven looked back at Jessica and Billie. He had a funny, help-less look on his face. He said nothing, but his eyes were shocked and scared.

Billie held Jessica tighter. Jessica could feel her sobbing now, too.

Seconds later two medics ran by them with a stretcher. Mike was strapped down under blan-kets. His face was white. One of the medics ran up to Jessica.

"Your husband's in bad shape, ma'am," he said. "You want to follow us to the hospital?"

She didn't hear the last part of what the medic said to her. She felt that funny distance again. Everything seemed far away, like she was watching herself from the outside. This man wasn't talking to her. *Husband?* But she was only eighteen years old, a college freshman, her parents' little girl . . .

"Ma'am, are you okay?"

The medic shook her by the arm. He turned to Billie. "You take care of her. She's in pretty bad shape herself."

Two police cars pulled in front of the ambulance, and the three vehicles sped out of the parking lot with their sirens wailing. Jessica listened to them cross the town toward the hospital, until the sound faded and she could hear nothing but the cicadas whirring in the trees.

She wriggled out of Billie's arms. But instead of walking to her car to follow the ambulance, she went back inside the apartment building. She pushed through the crowd of gawking and whispering neighbors in the lobby and went up to her own apartment.

Jessica closed the door behind her and looked around the room, at the couch where she and Mike used to eat Chinese food and make out, ignoring the videos they'd rented; at the kitchen table where they'd had coffee together each morning; at the empty vase that had bloomed with so many roses. But she felt nothing. *It's over.*

There was a knock. The doorknob rattled.

"Jess, are you in there?" It was Billie.

Jessica sniffed and got herself together. "Yeah, I'm in here, Billie. I'm all right. But look, I just want to be alone for a while, okay?"

"You sure you don't need me?"

"I'm sure."

"Well, I'll be in my apartment," Billie said. "I know you need time alone, Jess. I know you've had a horrible shock. But Steven is going to need your help. I'm going to start calling lawyers for him. Try to get yourself together. We have a lot ahead of us."

Jessica could feel herself starting to lose control again. "Okay, Billie. That's a good idea. I'll just be in here—"

Her dam of emotions was beginning to cave in. She bit her lip, waiting for Billie's footsteps to fade down the hall. Then she sank to the floor and let the tears fall.

"Tom, please."

This time Elizabeth wasn't taking no for an answer. "There's something else. Something bigger than the secret society. I can feel it. Please tell me."

Elizabeth pulled a folded piece of paper out of her pocket. She smoothed it and slid it in front of Tom. It was a photocopy of a photograph.

Recently she had spent an afternoon in the library. While Tom thought she was researching the secret society story, Elizabeth had actually been investigating her reporting partner. She'd looked up an old SVU newspaper interview with Tom when he was quarterback of the team. And it was incredible, simply incredible.

In the team photo Tom knelt front and center with the football in his hands. But it wasn't the Tom that Elizabeth knew, the darkly handsome, sensitive Tom, the one you had to look at two or three times before you realized just how attractive he really was. This Tom had a cocky glare and the arrogant aren't-I-good-looking-and-don't-I-know-it grin of a movie star. In the interview he had said he had only one passion: football. When asked what he planned to do after college, he answered, Play football.

"Who's that?" Elizabeth asked.

Tom just peered at the picture and shook his head. "What a waste."

"Where is that man?" she asked.

"Dead and buried," Tom murmured.

"Who killed him?"

Tom held up his hands. He tried to make it seem like a joke, but his eyes were filled with sadness. "Okay, okay, supersleuth. I'll try to explain. But I can't talk here," he said, looking around.

Tom set his gaze on her face. There was so much feeling in his eyes, she knew at last he was going to let her in. At last.

They stared at each other, unblinking. "It's true there's a lot you don't know. A lot I've never told anyone. Ever."

"Let's go." She took his hand, feeling a tingle of warmth at the touch of his skin.

As they began walking across campus to Tom's place Elizabeth barely noticed the sirens wailing in the distance.

The ringing of the telephone cut through the air in Celine's and Elizabeth's dorm room like a knife. An hour before, William had turned to Celine and stared at her for a long while, as if contemplating whether to kiss her. Then he'd whirled and flown out the door, leaving Celine licking her lips in a vacuum of silence and disappointment. Now Celine flounced over to the phone, sure it would be William to say he was sorry. *All men are the same. They always come crawling back,* she assured herself.

She reached the phone but let it ring three more times. This was part of the Boudreaux credo: Always keep them waiting—never let them think you *want* or *need* anything. She glanced at herself in the mirror, very happy with what she saw there.

"Hello?" she said in a soft, sexy drawl, trying her best to sound bored and enticing all at once.

"Celine, it's Jessica."

Celine sighed.

"Jessica Wakefield."

"Yes." Celine sighed again, exasperated.

"I need to talk to Elizabeth," Jessica said abruptly. She sounded strange, nervous and out of breath.

38

Celine smiled cruelly. Her roomie's twin sister seemed on the verge of tears. *Boy trouble,* she thought.

"The princess is at a sleepover," Celine said.

Jessica was sobbing. Celine could hear it clearly now.

"What's the matter?" Celine asked, trying to load sympathy into her words.

"Mike . . . Mike's been . . ."

Ho-hum, Celine thought. She had been right. Boy trouble.

"Something happened to Mike. He's been—"

"Yes?"

"Shot."

Celine was startled. *My, my,* she thought. *Now this is something new.*

"I'm at my brother's," Jessica continued in a ragged voice. "I mean, my brother's not here. They took him . . . Just tell her."

They took her brother? Who's *they?* Celine perked up, suddenly very interested. Maybe she should have moved in on Steven Wakefield herself, she mused. She hated to let all the interesting ones slip through her fingers.

"I might have an idea where your sister is," Celine said. "You sit tight, sugar. Let me do some checking."

As soon as she hung up Celine dialed William's number. "William, it's me," she purred when he answered. "Any sign of Elizabeth yet?"

"She'll turn up," he snapped.

"Well, well, well," Celine said. "Maybe I should come over and help you lick your wounds."

"I don't think so," he said.

"But William, I just heard the most interesting piece of news."

"Don't play with me, Celine."

"Believe me, honey, this is no play. This is right up your alley. Something about Elizabeth's brother, Steven. Something about Jessica Wakefield's husband, Mike. Something about a gun. And something about someone getting shot. I'll give you a hint: it wasn't their brother."

Celine could practically hear William's brain working.

"I'll be there in a minute," William said, then hung up.

Jessica sat on the couch in the living room of her and Mike's apartment. She'd been sitting all night like a woman chiseled out of granite. She looked through the double glass doors at the harvest moon. In her lap she held their wedding photograph, the one the owner of the diner had taken at their wedding dinner outside of Las Vegas. They were standing in front of a jukebox, their arms around each other. Mike, looking dangerously handsome, with his thick dark hair, jaw cut from granite, piercing eyes, and serious muscles behind his T-shirt, and Jessica, the ideal California blonde, were so perfect together, they could have done a Levi's ad.

If she ever had a question about how passionately they'd once felt for each other, all she had to do was look at the picture.

Every now and then Jessica heard a motorcycle rumble down the street, and she jumped, half-expecting Mike to come barreling through the door and sweep her up in his arms. At first the thought made her feel charged with excitement. But then she began to wonder. If Mike could really come back and sweep her away again, was that what she would truly want?

But Jessica didn't know if Mike ever could. She didn't even know if he was going to live.

What she did know was that she should go to the hospital and see him. It wasn't a matter of what she wanted to do anymore. It was her responsibility. After all, she was his wife.

The thought made Jessica proud. Not the thought that she was Mike McAllery's wife, but that she would do something just because she was *somebody's* wife. Because she was responsible. She'd been taking more of the load for their marital problems than she thought she should have. But it had seemed like the adult thing to do. Now Jessica understood that she could afford to carry the burden of blame because she was responsible.

"Responsible," Jessica repeated. In the past people had called her a lot of things, but never *responsible*.

She stood up and eyed the car keys on the table. She started to pick them up, but then she stopped. *Pick them up,* she commanded herself. *Pick up those keys.* She lifted the key ring, held them at full arm's length distance, and followed them to the door. She turned the knob, drew back the door, and took one step into the hallway.

Then she whirled around and hopped back into the apartment.

I can't do it. I just can't force myself to see Mike. Maybe I'm not as trustworthy as I thought.

She went to the phone and stared at it. Who to call . . . who to call. She felt so alone, as though there was no one left out there at all interested in hearing from her, much less helping her. She'd already tried calling Elizabeth, but all she got was Celine. Celine had said she'd try to track Elizabeth down, but from what Elizabeth had told her about Celine, she lied more easily than she told the truth.

She tried Steven's number. Billie picked up, out of breath.

"Hello!"

"Billie?" Jessica asked.

"Oh, *Jessica*! I was just waiting for some lawyer to call me back."

"I should get off, then," Jessica said in a small voice.

"You okay, Jess?"

"I'm hanging in. Look, you need this phone clear. I'll talk to you later. Bye, Billie."

Jessica hung up. It wasn't Billie she needed. Billie had her own hands full with Steven being in jail. No, she needed someone who knew her, someone who she could count on no matter what.

Jessica picked up the phone and shakily punched in her parents' number. She was so nervous, she misdialed twice. *They don't know anything about what's been going on,* she told herself. *They don't even know I'm married . . . they don't even know Mike McAllery exists.*

The phone rang. Once. Twice.

She began to tremble. How could she begin to explain that Mike not only existed, but he was her husband? And not only her husband, but the victim of a gunshot from Steven, their son? What would she say about what she'd been doing all these weeks? Where would she begin?

Jessica slammed down the phone before it rang again. There was too much to tell. She didn't think she had it in her. *But no matter how this all turns out, they'll hear about it somehow. Soon it's going to be all over the news—the papers, the television. I'd rather Mom and Dad found out about all this from me than some newscaster.*

She picked up the phone and dialed again. This time it took just one try. One ring . . . two rings . . . three rings . . . four rings . . .

"Hello . . ."

"Hello, M-Mom?" Jessica stammered.

". . . you have reached the Wakefield residence . . ."

"No!" Jessica shouted into the phone. "I don't want to talk to a stupid answering machine!"

Suddenly Jessica remembered. Her parents were on a cruise in the Caribbean. It was a birthday surprise her father had given her mother. They'd be gone another week.

Now what am I going to do? she thought in a panic.

Tom had pondered this moment a thousand times. Walking toward his room with Elizabeth, he remembered how sure he'd been that it could never happen.

But looking at her, feeling her hand in his, he knew it was right. After all these weeks he had to bare his soul to her. He had to unload everything. *Everything,* he reminded himself. *My life, my family. Everything.*

He led Elizabeth into his room and kicked the door shut behind him. The place was a pigsty, but he was too focused to care.

All he could think was, *Tell her.*

He swept away two piles of clothes and two chairs appeared. Both of them sat, unable to talk, as if they were in a trance.

"Elizabeth," he began, his heart pounding. But the campus police scanner Tom kept on his desk squawked. Elizabeth jumped.

"Sorry," he said sheepishly.

"Is this how you get your fast-breaking news stories, Mr. Watts?" Elizabeth sat back in her chair, laughing nervously.

"You never know what could be happening out there."

"It's the last way on earth I'd ever want to hear bad news," Elizabeth said.

She looked nervous. Tom began to have second thoughts. *Tough,* he said to himself. *Enough diversions. She's got to know. If we're ever going to have a chance to be together* . . .

"Elizabeth," he started again.

Again the scanner squawked.

"Let me turn that thing off," Tom said, now annoyed. He reached for the knob. Then he froze. Elizabeth leapt to her feet.

"Attention all units," the dispatcher called. "Man near campus . . . shots fired . . . suspect in custody, SVU student, Caucasian male, six foot one inch, dark hair . . . registered name, Steven Wakefield . . ."

Todd stood in the middle of the quad and looked up for shooting stars. After the scene with Lauren, he'd trudged to Mark Gathers's room. They were supposed to have another meeting with the dean tomorrow. Todd wanted to get their stories straight before they went.

But Mark wasn't there, and from the note he'd left, he wouldn't be back anytime soon.

Todd,
*   It's time to wake up to reality. We're nothing but sacrificial lambs. Like I said, we've already been pushed over the edge of the cliff. It's just a matter of time before we hit the bottom. I'll be gone for a few days. I'm looking into other possibilities for the future. If I were you, I'd do the same. No one cares, buddy. It's every man for himself.*
*   Mark*

Todd had headed downstairs and out into the night. He couldn't spend another night watching the walls of his room closing in on

46

him. The streets around the quad were quiet. It must have been past three in the morning. The last of the frat parties would have broken up.

So no one cares, huh? Todd thought. He crumpled the note into a ball, faked a dribble, pumped, and shot a jumper toward the trash can ten feet away. Air ball. The paper rolled into the shadows.

Todd laughed sadly to himself. "Figures," he said.

Elizabeth cares, a voice in his head told him.

He remembered the last time he'd looked for shooting stars. It was September, the night before he and Elizabeth left home for SVU. They'd celebrated their "last date." The last night of their old life. They'd gone to all their favorite places, beginning with a romantic dinner at the Box Tree Café and ending with a milk shake with the old high school crowd at the Dairi Burger.

Then they'd driven to a spot high in the hills above the town, just the two of them. They'd wrapped themselves in a blanket and whispered to each other about their hopes and dreams, for themselves and for each other. They must have wished on a hundred shooting stars that night.

"Who knows where we'll be a month from now," Todd had said to her.

"Are you scared?" she'd asked him.

"What is there to be scared of?" he'd reassured her. "Don't think about what's ending. Think about what's beginning."

It was the last time Todd could remember taking the time to relax and stare at the sky, and dare himself to dream.

Everything changed the day after he dumped Elizabeth for Lauren. Thinking back, he wasn't sure why he did it. Sure, Lauren was good looking and sexy. She treated him like he was something special. And, he had to admit this was part of it, she wanted to have sex with him.

But she wasn't Elizabeth. She wasn't as smart, she wasn't as funny. She didn't own any Save the Earth T-shirts. Lauren didn't seem to care about anything except Todd Wilkins: staying with him, catering to his every need. At first Todd had liked it. He was a big man on campus; he felt he deserved it. He'd gotten frustrated with Elizabeth for worrying about her classes and crusades so much. He thought she'd lost sight of what really mattered.

Maybe it was me who lost his sight, Todd thought. Lauren was in love with what Todd was supposed to be, but not what he was. She didn't want a guy who was insecure, so she just didn't deal with that part.

And now Elizabeth was running around campus with that Watts guy, investigating everyone and everything. *Investigating me!* He had to admire her. And now look at him, Mr. BMOC. The higher you climb, the farther you fall. . . .

Craning his neck upward, Todd didn't think of Lauren anymore but only of what he'd said to her about Elizabeth, that maybe he shouldn't have broken up with her. He'd never allowed himself to say it seriously before. And the way it just slipped out, unplanned—it was his heart talking. And maybe it was right. Wasn't that what they always said? The mind *thinks* it knows everything, but the heart knows the truth?

There! Out of the corner of his eye, he saw a shooting star. Todd closed his eyes and wished . . . There. He had done it. For the first time in his life he had actually wished to turn back the clock. To have a second chance.

To have Elizabeth back.

Chapter
Three

_____

Steven lay on the narrow bed in his cell, rubbing his wrists. It was hardly a bed—more like a slab of wood too short to stretch out on. Across the aisle, practically right next to him, some old drunken geezer was snoring so loudly Steven could hardly hear himself think. He could actually feel the vibrations rumbling in the bunk springs below him.

And the old guy smelled—like sickly-sweet liquor and ancient, unwashed clothes.

Steven tried not to breathe in too hard or listen too closely. Prison! It all came to him at once: the steel bars, the tiny window near the ceiling, the clanking of opening and closing doors echoing down the long hallway. He felt like he was in one of those prison movies. Except that the real thing was worse than he ever imagined. In the movies the hero's stomach didn't actually rumble with hunger. And the hero didn't feel how suffocating it was not to be able to stretch his legs or take three steps without running into a concrete wall. And his wrists didn't sting from the pinching handcuffs. And Steven couldn't just get up and walk out when the movie was over.

And the humiliation of it. The police had taken everything away: the watch that his father had given him for high school graduation, the belt Billie had bought him last Christmas. Even his wallet. Steven had nothing on him to prove who he was. All he had was a serial number: 11231, Inmate Wakefield, accused murderer.

Murderer!

"I don't believe it," he said to himself.

The old man grumbled in his sleep and rolled over. Steven gagged on an invisible wave of bad air.

"Ugh," he said, rolling the opposite way. His nose pressed against the gray, cold, concrete wall.

Would this be his view before he fell asleep for the rest of his life? Steven had no idea about Mike's condition. He didn't know if Mike had pulled through. For all he knew, Mike had died, and the district attorney was drawing up papers for first-degree murder charges at this very moment. Steven was pre-law. He knew the penalty: life imprisonment, with no parole.

Even though Steven had thought sometimes that he'd like to kill Mike, he knew he would never be able to live with himself if Mike died. When Billie had visited him an hour ago, she still didn't have any news.

Billie—would he ever get to hold her again? They'd pressed their hands together on the bulletproof glass that separated them in the visiting room. It was strange to talk by telephone to someone who was five inches away.

"I hate him," he had said to Billie. "But I didn't mean to hurt him. I was just trying to protect my baby sister."

"I know," Billie said. "We'll get you out of here. I promise."

Steven had wanted to believe her, but he wasn't sure he even deserved for everything to work out. He disliked Mike intensely, but never enough to really hurt him . . . to kill him. What had he done?

Steven saw the terrible scene all over again, more vivid in his mind than the concrete wall in front of him: Mike barreling in, Mike's hands on his throat. He felt the cold metal of the gun. The explosion. The smell of gunpowder. All that smoke. Billie and Jessica watching him being led away in handcuffs. Then the long ride in the back of the police car. The loud clank of the door to his cell being slammed behind him.

Still, there was a nagging question. *Who pulled the trigger?* he wondered. He honestly didn't know. *Was it me or him?*

Elizabeth sat beside Jessica on a long bench at the police station waiting for word about Steven. She slipped her arm through her twin's. Everyone who walked by, from the police officers to the janitors, stopped and did a double take at the identical twins. Both wore their golden blond hair loose and long over their shoulders, and both sat hunched on the bench the same way. The only clue people had that they weren't seeing double was that Elizabeth was still in her black evening gown from the charity ball, while Jessica was wearing one of her brother's ratty sweatshirts.

Jessica entwined her fingers in Elizabeth's and told her haltingly about Steven's scuffle with Mike, the gun suddenly going off.

"You know what the worst part of this whole mess is?" Jessica said, her voice trembling. "As I sat there waiting for the ambulance, I thought Mike was dead, and part of me actually felt . . . *relieved.*"

Elizabeth had no reply.

The last time she had seen Jessica with Mike, Jessica looked happy and beautiful. Elizabeth had always been sure that Mike was a violent criminal, the scum of the earth. But that night she'd begun to have second thoughts. She actually remembered thinking that married life suited her twin.

Then just a few days later she'd gone back to their apartment and found the door flung wide open and the floor covered with turned-over furniture and broken glass. Jessica, red faced and exhausted from crying, had been clutching at the side of the bed, terrified that Mike might come back.

It didn't make sense to Elizabeth. She'd never heard of anything like it. One night Jessica and Mike looked like they were standing arm in arm on top of the world, and the next they looked like they'd fallen through the cracks and landed in purgatory. Now, though, it seemed like they'd taken the express through purgatory and gone straight to hell.

Mike had tried to kill their brother. What could Elizabeth say?

"Everything will work out, Jess," was all she could think of.

"But with Mom and Dad out of town, and

Steven stuck in jail . . ." Jessica cried.

"We'll get him out," Elizabeth assured her.

Just then Billie walked into the room. Her eyes were red. Tissue shreds leaked out between her fingers. She stopped in front of them and looked from one twin to the other, like she couldn't tell them apart either. Her eyes filled with tears.

"Come and sit down," Elizabeth said, patting the bench next to her. Billie sat and leaned wearily against Elizabeth.

"They're holding Steven for attempted murder," Billie finally said.

"Attempted *murder*!" both twins cried.

"The district attorney isn't giving an inch. He said that SVU students aren't above the law and that he wants to make an example of Steven."

"How much is bail?" Elizabeth asked.

"We won't know until the hearing tomorrow," Billie said.

"Tomorrow!" Jessica wailed. "Why not now? I thought he wouldn't have to spend the night in jail!"

"It could have been tomorrow," Billie said. "But the D.A. is making this more complicated. He says he's waiting to see if Mike is going to pull through."

Elizabeth asked, although she already knew

56

the answer: "And if he doesn't?"

Billie's lips quivered. "Then it wouldn't be attempted murder. It would be murder."

All three sat back, dazed and overwhelmed.

"He can tough it out," Billie finally said, getting herself together. "It's not jail I'm worried about. It's just that . . . that . . ." She turned to Jessica. "Jess, he feels so *bad* about all this!" She started crying again. "You know what a conscience your brother has. He actually *thinks* he's a murderer."

Now Jessica started crying, too. Elizabeth put out her arms and held them both against her.

"I'm not doing you two any good," Billie said, sniffling. "I better go home and call some more lawyers. I have a feeling we're going to need all the legal advice we can get. Want a lift home, Jessica?"

"Home?" Jessica said, suddenly unsure of where that was supposed to be.

"I'll take Jess back," Elizabeth said. "We still need to talk."

"Okay." Billie stood. But she didn't move, as if her feet were glued to the floor.

"Billie?" Elizabeth asked. "Are you all right?"

"What? Yeah, I think so. It's just I—I guess I don't know if I want to be alone right now."

"Then stay with us," Jessica said. "Sit back down."

"No," Billie said, drying her eyes. "No. Thanks. I really should get home. I have the names of a couple of lawyers. Steven's depending on me. I'll see you later."

"I'll call you," Elizabeth said.

"Okay," Billie said, smiling bravely, then left.

Elizabeth put her arm around her sister's shoulders. "I guess it's just us."

"The Fabulous Wakefield Twins," Jessica said.

They both tried to laugh, then gave up.

"Jess, I wanted to ask you something." Elizabeth looked her twin straight in the eye. "What are you going to do now?"

"Right now I'm going to get a super-deluxe burrito with cheese, guacamole, and sour cream. No, nix that. A triple-cheese pepperoni pizza. On second thought . . . Forget it." Jessica put her hands on her stomach. "There's no way I could eat."

"I mean about *Mike*, Jess."

Jessica murmured something under her breath.

"What's that?"

"I said I knew you were asking about Mike."

"So?" Elizabeth pressed on.

"So nothing."

"Nothing?"

Jessica hung her head. "I won't see him, if that's what you mean. I can't." She gave Elizabeth a helpless look. "What am I doing?

58

I'm only eighteen. I shouldn't even be married."

Elizabeth raised her eyebrows. "But you *are*," she said. "You can't just pretend he doesn't exist. And besides, I think you should see him. I don't know—maybe you even kind of owe it to him to see him."

"Owe it to him!" Jessica cried.

"It would be different if he weren't your *husband*, Jess," Elizabeth reminded her. "If you weren't his *wife*."

Jessica stared into her hands. Elizabeth could tell she was really struggling with this. She knew her twin wanted to do the right thing, but the problem was, what was the right thing? What do you take care of first? Yourself or your obligations?

"I'm not talking about staying with him for the rest of your life, Jess," Elizabeth said.

"Then what *are* you suggesting?" Jessica asked.

Elizabeth tightened her reassuring grip on her sister's shoulder. "Jessica, I'm not angry with you now. I'm here to support you. But not too long ago, you made the decision to marry Mike—"

"I wanted it then. I loved him!" Jessica cried.

"Well, you can't just pretend it never happened." Elizabeth looked into the eyes that mirrored her own. "Jessica, you have to stop thinking about yourself right now. Steven is in jail for shooting *your husband*. I'm not saying you should stay with him. But right now he's in the hospital. He's fighting for his life. Not seeing him now might be a decision you'll always regret."

Jessica seemed to be caving in. Her eyes looked stormy. Elizabeth could tell her twin was fighting a war inside herself. She decided to back off. She was sure Jessica would come to the right decision on her own.

Elizabeth found a quarter in her purse and pressed it into Jessica's palm. "Will you at least call the hospital?"

Jessica moaned.

"Please," Elizabeth persisted.

She gave Jessica a helpful little shove off the bench. Jessica trudged to the pay phone. As she dropped in the quarter she looked back, her face stricken with fear and indecision. It was as if she were screaming across the police station lobby, "Somebody please take me away from all this!"

Elizabeth knew Jessica was begging her to be the one to take her away. As different as they were, and as much time as they had spent apart since they'd arrived at college, there was an incredible bond between them. They were identical twins, and in the past when one of them was in real trouble, the other had been there in a flash to help.

Jessica looked even gloomier when she came back to the bench.

"Well?" Elizabeth asked.

"He's still in intensive care."

"But is he better?"

"He's unconscious," Jessica said, her voice wavering, her eyes brimming with tears. "They don't know if he'll ever wake up."

Celine rolled over, purring like a kitten. But when her arm landed on an empty bed, she gingerly opened one eye, shielding her face from the morning light pouring in through the window.

"William, where are you?" she called out.

She heard a grunt from across the room. She opened the other eye and saw William sitting fully dressed on the edge of Elizabeth's un-slept-in bed with a drink in his hand. A silver flask lay empty on its side next to him.

"You're in the wrong bed," Celine said in her sexy, slinky little girl's voice. "Why don't you come back to mine?"

"I don't think so," William snapped. "I never imagined you as the cuddly type the morning after, Celine."

Celine felt like kicking him. But she forced herself to spread on a syrupy smile. "Looks are deceiving, William. In the right circumstances I can be almost anything your little heart desires."

When William didn't answer, Celine sighed and reached for her cigarettes. Her head momentarily evaporated behind a cloud of smoke.

"Okay, so now what?" she asked, her Southern drawl all but gone.

"Now," William replied, "we wait for Elizabeth to get home. And then I convince her that I have nothing to do with the secret society."

Celine laughed.

"I wouldn't laugh," William barked. "You'll help me convince her or you'll find yourself in more trouble than even you could imagine."

William's perfect, cool composure was growing ragged around the edges. "Convince her?" Celine demanded. "Not likely. One thing I've learned about Miss Goody Two-Shoes is that when she sets her mind on something, she doesn't let go. And she certainly doesn't take advice from me." She took a deep draw on her cigarette. "I'm afraid that the only way you could keep that girl quiet would be to get rid of her completely." Celine laughed again.

This time a look came over William's face that did make Celine stop laughing. He stared unseeing out the window.

"You see, my dearest?" William said softly. "You're giving yourself away. Not that we didn't already know the scheming heart that lurks behind that sweet Southern belle expression."

William laughed coldly and turned his ice-blue eyes on her. "Celine, you're already more of an accomplice than you thought."

Tom leaned back in his chair. He had wanted to go down to the police station with Elizabeth, but she insisted on going alone.

Wherever he looked—at the computer screen on his desk, at the telephone, even at his own reflection in the mirror—all he saw was Elizabeth's face, the shock of hearing her brother's name on the police scanner, her blue-green eyes rimmed with tears. His first attempts to comfort her had been so inadequate. What he'd wanted to do was simply take her in his arms and make everything better. *Everything's going to be all right,* he longed to tell her—about this thing with her brother, about the secret society, about everything. *You're not alone. I'll always be there for you. Always . . .*

But, of course, he hadn't said anything like that. He'd said, "Can I go with you?" like he was the one who needed the comfort. Like he was afraid to be alone.

He looked out the window at the dawning day. This time it wasn't Elizabeth he was seeing; this time it was the faces of his family— his parents, his older sister, his little brother. It was getting harder and harder to remember what they looked like. So much time had passed.

Tom pulled out the lowest drawer in his desk and dug into a deep pile of papers. He felt around on the bottom of the drawer, then found what he was looking for and held it in his lap. It was a photograph, a group shot of the last time his entire family had been together. It was a good-bye party they'd thrown for him when he first went off to school, off to SVU. Tom's hands shook. His stomach cramped up. Their absence was like a physical pain. He still missed them so much it was like they'd been ripped out of his body. He thought of them every day. And the wound wouldn't heal.

You're alone, he told himself.

He'd always hoped Elizabeth needed him. But he couldn't lie to himself anymore. It was the other way around. He needed her. And he didn't want to need anyone. It was like a curse. The last people he had needed vanished off the face of the earth. To be needed by Tom Watts had become a death sentence. Unfortunately, every minute Elizabeth was away from him his need for her grew.

There was one thing standing between Tom and Elizabeth. One thing preventing him from finding out whether she could ever love him back.

And that was Tom. He was protecting the wound of an old and secret past. And if he didn't let go, he could never have her.

He had to try.

Outside, day was breaking like a gray smear on the horizon. The first morning birds began to warble in the trees. Tom grabbed his jacket and headed out his door for Dickenson Hall, Elizabeth's dorm.

Jessica stood under the hot water a long time. She told herself a long, hot shower would do her good. Her last shower in this apartment.

Everything she did was for the last time. The last time she opened the fridge. The last time she made the bed. The last time she put away the dishes. She'd reminded herself to look hard and commit it all to memory. As though all this was already something decided, something over and done with, written in stone. There was no looking back. It was definitely the end of something. But the question was, What was it the beginning of?

She turned off the water. She had been right about the shower. She felt more like herself already. She *looked* better, anyway. She got dressed in jeans and a white T-shirt, glanced at herself in the mirror, and felt even better. Her gold hair shone in the sunlight. Her eyes were still red from all that crying, but some things just couldn't be helped.

Books in hand, she left the apartment for what she hoped would be the last time and started toward the stairs. She found herself face-to-face with Billie.

"Hi," Jessica said, feeling a little bad that she was changed and showered while Billie still looked haggard with worry. "How's Steven?"

"That's what I was coming to tell you. I just got off the phone with the district attorney. They're going to set bail at the hearing this afternoon. I was just going to wash up and get down to the courthouse. But no matter what, Steven will be home by dinner."

"Thank God," Jessica said.

"We're going to get through this, Jess. Don't worry."

Jessica threw Billie a disbelieving glance. It seemed like this was still the beginning of the trouble. There was so much she still had to deal with.

"But who will represent Steven in court?" Jessica asked.

"I took care of everything," Billie said reassuringly. "A public defender will represent him. Somebody who was highly recommended. A friend of a friend."

"I feel better already," Jessica said, relieved.

"So," Billie said. "You going to the hospital to see Mike?"

"Not exactly," Jessica began. She paused. "Actually, I'm going to class," she said, as if she couldn't believe it herself. "You are?"

For what seemed like the millionth time in the last twenty-four hours, Jessica's eyes filled with tears. She didn't think she had any left. "I don't know what I'm doing, Billie," she said, keeping down a sob. "I loved Mike so much— or at least I *thought* I did. I tried to do what was right. But now all I want is to be a college student again."

"Jess, I think it's great, your going to class and everything. But don't you think you should—"

"Billie," Jessica interrupted. Her eyes had dried up. She straightened and held her books against her chest. "I just can't face seeing Mike again. It's all over between us. I'm going to file for divorce. Once Steven is out of jail, I want to forget all this ever happened.

I never want to see Mike McAllery again."
She pulled away and started to drift down the
hall. "I'm moving back into my dorm room.
Call me as soon as you know anything about
Steven." She ran out the door and down to
the parking lot.

Elizabeth pulled her Jeep into a space in
front of Dickenson Hall. She'd never felt so exhausted. It wasn't only the sleepless night.
Sleep was the least of her worries. She needed
to be strong and composed for Jessica, but
now she felt herself crumbling. Everything was
happening at once. Jessica and Steven, Mike,
William.

And of course there was Tom Watts.

She couldn't begin to sort out all things she
felt for him.

But could she trust him?

Would he ever explain to her who he really
was? What had happened to him that had
changed him so much? Who had hurt him so
badly that he couldn't reach out to anyone?

As she approached the doorway to her dorm
a hand reached out of the shadows and grabbed
her by the shoulder. A figure in a hooded sweatshirt stepped out. Elizabeth shrieked and in-
stinctively raised her fists.

*   *   *

"It's me, Elizabeth." Tom pulled back the hood of his sweatshirt. "I'm sorry. I didn't mean to scare you."

Elizabeth put her hand to her throat. She took a deep, steadying breath. "I'm okay."

Tom gazed at her with concern in his eyes. She looked beautiful to him, but tired. She looked drawn and pale and so fragile.

"Are you okay?" he asked. "How's your sister?"

Elizabeth gave a tiny shrug. Her eyes filled with tears, and he knew she was fighting to keep control.

He wanted to take her in his arms. Just hold her and let her cry as long as she needed to. *I love you,* he'd whisper in her ear. *I'd do anything for you.*

"I better go up to my room and pull myself together," Elizabeth said, a tremble in her voice. He could tell she had to cry and wanted to do it alone. "Did you need me for something?"

Tom stared at her, caught in her gaze. He searched his brain for the words to begin the speech he'd prepared. "I . . . I, uh . . ."

That was when it dawned on him. Here she was, her sister's husband shot to death for all he knew, her brother in custody, and he was going to tell her his long tale of woe? She was clearly exhausted, shaken, holding on to her composure by a thread, and he was

69

going to dump his life story on her?

It seemed ridiculous. Crazy. Totally selfish.

Instead he just reached out and took hold of her hand. He felt a tingle climb up his arm at the touch of her skin. "You go to sleep," he said gently. "Try not to worry. If there's anything I can do, let me know."

Her eyes were enormous and shiny with tears that threatened to spill over at any second. "Thanks, Tom," she said, and stepped into the dorm.

"Chicken," Tom muttered to himself as he walked away.

As Jessica drove through town toward the SVU campus, she felt strangely relieved. *I never want to see Mike McAllery again.* Now that she'd finally spoken those words aloud, she felt a wave of relief wash through her. She had said that before, or something like it, when she'd thought she'd seen him with other women. She hadn't meant it then, but she knew she meant it now. She meant it more than anything in the world.

She flipped on the car radio. Out of the speakers came music that reminded her of a time before SVU, a time when she was flirtatious and free, hanging out with the Sweet Valley High crowd at the Dairi Burger back home. Life was simpler then.

She thought of her first euphoric weeks at college—moving into her dorm room with Isabella, getting asked out by practically every gorgeous man on campus. The time when she was just a normal college student on top of the world.

She turned up the radio and sang to herself, glancing at her reflection in the rearview mirror. Her eyes were clearing. She felt welling up inside her a tiny glimmer of hope.

But then the song was cut short. The urgent voice of a newscaster broke though the melody: "A shooting occurred last night at an apartment complex near campus. An unidentified man has been taken to the hospital and is in critical condition in intensive care. An SVU student is in police custody. We'll bring you more on this late-breaking news throughout the day. . . ."

Jessica let the car roll to a stop in the middle of the road. The traffic flew by on either side, cars honking, screaming drivers shaking angry fists. Her eyes filled with tears, and just for a moment she felt anger well up inside her. But then something else beat it back. It was fear.

"All right, all you thieves and mother beaters and baby snatchers! Up and at 'em!"

Steven sat bolt upright on his slab of soggy mattress. He thought a train was derailing on the other side of the wall. But it was only the jailer dragging his nightstick along the bars of all the cells.

"Get up, you muggers. And oh, what have we here? I believe we have our first *university* student. Okay, listen up, it's exercise hour. Crack of dawn. Best time of the day. And then maybe our little visitor from the *university* will give us a lecture. What's your major, Mr. Wakefield?"

Steven squinted up through the bright light at the warden. The guy was twisted. He actually seemed to be enjoying his job.

"What's your *major*, Wakefield?"

Steven murmured his major under his breath.

"What's that? Say it nice and loud for all your new friends to hear."

"Prelaw," Steven said, hardly above a whisper.

"Louder!"

"Prelaw!" Steven shouted.

The cavernous jail echoed with the hysterical laughter of twenty men.

"Hey, boy, maybe I can get some advice!" one of them yelled.

"He must not be much of a student. Look where he is!"

Another round of laughter.

Steven shrank into the back of his cell.

72

"Okay, boys. Exercise time!"

Steven followed men of all shapes and sizes and ages out into the bare courtyard. The walls were high and topped by billows of barbed wire. The sky, or the little he could see of it, was just lightening. He took deep breaths of the cool air. It hadn't been even a day since he'd been outside, but it felt like years.

Out of nowhere a basketball hit him in the head and bounced to the ground.

"Hey, lawyer, let's play ball!"

Nine of the biggest and ugliest men he had ever seen were gathered under the basket.

Steven winced. But he forced himself to play. Otherwise those nine men might decide he was the game.

"So, whatdya think?" one of them asked as he dribbled past Steven.

"Of what?" Steven said, already out of breath.

"My case."

"What did you do?"

"Beat up a kid."

"How old was he?"

"Oh, about your age."

The man leaned a shoulder into Steven's chest, leapt, and jammed the ball through the basket and off Steven's head.

"Nice one, schoolboy!" another man said, shoving him as he ran back up the court.

"That's jailbirds two, lawyers nothing!" one of them yelled. "Nothing, big shot. As in zero, zilch, *nada*."

"Hey, lawyer, you want to quit while you're behind?"

Please, Billie. Please Billie please, get me out of here.

"Hey, lawyer, I believe my friend is talking to you. You up for the challenge or you gonna quit like all you other mamma's boys up on that hill?"

"No way," Steven answered, racing back up the court. "Play ball!"

"Maybe the lawyer's all right," one of his teammates said. He came over to Steven to shake hands. Steven offered his hand, which was quickly engulfed and nearly crushed to a pulp. The man grinned down at him. He was missing half his teeth.

"Hey, boy, what'd you do to get in here?"

"Shot someone," Steven said.

The others stopped playing.

"Shot someone!" one of the men cried. "Get outa town. Who'd you shoot?"

"M-my sister's husband."

The others whistled and applauded. "All right! Right on!"

Steven's gap-toothed friend took him by the shoulders and aimed him at the others as if he were introducing him. "Hey, my man here may look a little funny, but he's all right. Dig it. I been wanting to shoot my brother-in-law for ten years! This guy's my kind of lawyer!"

Chapter Four

Celine Boudreaux was a first-class pebble in Elizabeth's shoe. She was a liar, a greedy consumer of men; she was self-absorbed, she smoked, she was a gossip, a snoop, and a slob. But the one positive thing about Celine was that she wouldn't wake from her catatonic slumber if a convoy of bulldozers drove right past her bed. For that, this morning, Elizabeth was eternally grateful. All she wanted was to sneak inside, slip under her covers, give herself over to a good cry, and fall asleep into a far country a hemisphere away from all her cares. Maybe Kenya. She'd always wanted to see cheetahs in their natural habitat. She'd dream of going on safari in Africa.

And then when she woke up and was feeling better, she'd do some studying. She had a huge exam in three days. English. And she was only halfway through *Middlemarch*.

Elizabeth opened the door to her room quietly, praying the sleeping beast would not wake.

"Damn," Elizabeth muttered to herself.

Not only was Celine awake, she was standing by the window blowing smoke rings over Elizabeth's bed and wearing next to nothing—a small red thing she'd ordered from Victoria's Secret.

As soon as Elizabeth stepped into the room her eyes landed on something far worse. William White sat fully clothed on Elizabeth's desk.

Elizabeth stopped breathing. She could feel her blood pulsing in her temple. It was as if a criminal already convicted and sentenced had showed up in her room when he was supposed to be in prison. Or the devil himself on leave from hell. She'd forgotten that this criminal still had to be caught.

"What are you doing here?" she said slowly, not wanting to reveal the trauma he'd caused her.

"Elizabeth, you surprise me," William said. His gaze was less sharp than usual and his speech slightly slurred.

Is he drunk? Elizabeth wondered.

Celine took a wobbly step and collapsed on her bed.

He was, Elizabeth realized. They both were.

Elizabeth got ahold of her composure. She had

to stay calm. "William, please leave my room."

The expression on William's face changed. It went from sly and secretive to practically angelic, his ice blue eyes suddenly melting. But he didn't fool Elizabeth—not anymore. Anyone who could shift gears that quickly couldn't be believed, or trusted, ever again.

"Please, Elizabeth. We had a little misunderstanding last night—" William beseeched her.

"You could say that," Elizabeth replied coldly.

Celine called from her bed, "Are the two little lovebirds having their first fight?"

"Be quiet, Celine," William snarled.

"But sugar," Celine cooed, "such a change from the sweet nothings you whispered in my ear all night."

Elizabeth felt sick to her stomach. "Well, that's wonderful," she said ironically. "I can't think of two people who deserve each other more."

"Don't pay any attention to her," William said forcefully. He stepped toward Elizabeth and held out an apologetic hand. But he spoke sternly, like an angry father. "We've had a misunderstanding, and I'm here to work it out," he said, as if demanding it.

"Don't bother. There's nothing to work out," Elizabeth said quickly. She fixed her gaze on his. "I know who you are. I know what you've done. I can't believe I ever trusted you."

William dropped his hand. Elizabeth could practically feel the chilly wind blow as his eyes narrowed to slits and his tone turned cold.

"Quite a conclusion, Miss Wakefield."

"I know what I saw."

"And that's your only evidence?"

"It's enough."

He smiled. "You surprise me, Elizabeth," he said again. "I didn't think you were so gullible. I didn't think you could be swayed so easily. Let me guess. Tom Watts, am I right? He's the one who sent you on this wild-goose chase?"

Elizabeth folded her arms. "I'm not gullible," she whispered. "Not anymore. For the first time in a long while I'm seeing the truth."

"Okay. Then let me ask you a question," William said. "*If* there is in fact a secret society, and *if* I were in it, would I really be dumb enough to leave evidence sitting around in my bedroom?"

Elizabeth kept her face impassive.

"And another thing. Have you forgotten that Watts himself has a stake in how this turns out?"

William was losing his cool, Elizabeth realized. His perfect, precise manner was starting to come apart.

"Let me ask you something, Elizabeth. And be honest. Have you really ruled out Tom Watts?"

"I've heard enough of your lies," Elizabeth

said wearily. "I know the truth. I can't believe I've been so blind."

Without missing a beat, William stepped toward Elizabeth. Menace was written all over his face, but Elizabeth didn't give any ground.

"I thought you were special," William seethed, "but now I realize just how common you are. Even if I am what you say, you will never, I repeat *never* in your life be able to prove any of it."

William stormed by her and out the door without another word.

"So," Celine cooed, "I guess this means you two are breaking up?"

Todd sat reading an old *National Geographic* in the dean's waiting room. The chair enveloped him. It was like a throne, encasing him on all sides. Or was it more like an electric chair? His eyes passed over the article on white-water rafting without reading it. His eyes stuck, though, on one photograph, a spectacular scene of three rafts plunging over a waterfall. The men in the rafts were practically engulfed in the cascading torrents, holding their oars above their heads as they plunged over the edge.

I know just how you feel, he told the rafters in the picture.

Somewhere a clock ticktocked loudly. Todd

looked right and left. Where was Mark? Where was Lauren? Why was he going through this all alone? Where, he allowed himself to wonder, was Elizabeth?

The secretary came in and told Todd the dean was ready to see him. Todd stood and tugged with his finger at the knot of his tie; it had begun to feel like a noose. He tried to look confident as he walked into the dean's office.

"Sit down, young man," the dean said, pointing to a chair opposite his desk. He was short and bald and wore a bow tie and bottle-thick glasses. Next to the dean Todd looked like a superhuman giant: towering and tan and finely muscled, in the prime of his life. His whole life lay before him like a green pasture—a record-breaking career at SVU, maybe a few years playing pro basketball. As Todd sat a picture flashed before him: him defending against Michael Jordan in the NBA championship, the last seconds, game tied, Jordan goes up for a dunk, Todd leaps with him, both in the air, suspended; as Jordan brings the ball down like a hammer Todd extends his arm, gets a piece of the ball, which deflects into the screaming home crowd, and he and Michael tumble to the court in a tangle of arms and legs. The crowd leaps to its feet.

The dean cleared his throat.

The picture evaporated.

It just didn't seem right that all that would be shattered by a short, weaselly little guy in a bow tie.

"Is Mr. Gathers outside?" the dean asked.

"Mark won't be here," Todd murmured.

"Speak up, Mr. Wilkins."

Todd repeated himself.

"I see." That seemed to make the dean angrier. "I hate to see a student lose interest in his own destiny." He peered at Todd over his glasses. "As for you, the trustees will make a final decision about the state of your scholarship and eligibility by the end of next week," he pronounced. "In the meantime, you cannot attend practice or have anything to do with the SVU athletics department. You are temporarily suspended."

Suspended. The word reverberated through Todd's mind, echoing in his brain as if through a deep canyon.

The dean closed Todd's file and put it away. He flipped through his appointment book. But Todd didn't move. He felt his mouth moving, but he couldn't believe what he heard it saying.

"What about the school?"

"What about the school, Mr. Wilkins?" the dean asked, not even raising his head.

"I mean, shouldn't the school take some responsibility for all this?"

83

The dean took off his glasses and rubbed his eyes.

"I mean, I was just following the coaches' lead," Todd continued. "I didn't ask for anything. They offered. And I didn't know it was wrong to accept. That doesn't seem fair—"

"This isn't a hearing, Mr. Wilkins," the dean cut him off irritably. "You already had your chance to testify. I am just the trustees' messenger. So, if you'll excuse me."

"It just seems to me that the school—"

"The *school*, Mr. Wilkins, is none of your concern. The *school* will take care of itself. What *should* concern you is *your* future, not SVU's. You might pass on that advice to Mr. Gathers. Now good day, Mr. Wilkins."

"Elizabeth, I'm so glad to see you!"

Nina yanked Elizabeth into her room. She was still in her bathrobe, getting ready for classes.

When she got Elizabeth inside, Nina put her arms around her and hugged her. And Elizabeth found herself sagging into her friend's arms. For a brief moment everything she was worrying about—Jessica, Steven, Tom, William and the secret society—seemed to roll right off her shoulders. She hadn't known how much she was carrying until she let it all go. She felt a tear trickle down the side of her nose.

After William left her room, Elizabeth had the unbearable urge to confide in someone, to unload some of her burden. Nina was trustworthy, objective, and smart, and one of the best friends she'd ever had. So she had come straight here, even though it was still early. And now that she had Nina face-to-face, all she could do was collapse in her arms.

But as they broke apart Elizabeth realized she couldn't confide in Nina about everything. At least not yet. After all, the secret society had put Nina in the hospital and almost killed her friend, Bryan. It wasn't something she could be objective about.

"I'm so, so sorry about what happened," Nina said gently, still holding on to Elizabeth's hand.

"You heard?" Elizabeth asked.

"Just now. On the radio. I couldn't believe it."

Elizabeth nodded.

"I'm sure Steven is innocent. He has to be."

Elizabeth tried to talk but couldn't. She cleared her throat. "But he—he did shoot him," she said.

Nina's eyes widened in surprise.

"I mean, he was only defending himself. Mike had a gun, and . . . they fought. He was coming after Jess. And—"

Elizabeth felt like she was about to collapse. Nina embraced her again. "What a nightmare," she muttered.

85

"I wish it were." Elizabeth pulled away. "I wish I could wake up and it would be over." She wiped away her tears. "I'm sorry. I'm sorry to dump all this on you. Here." She handed over a bag of croissants.

Elizabeth had thought they'd have breakfast together. But to be honest, she didn't feel like eating at all. In fact, she couldn't remember the last time she'd had a meal. A few days ago it was the Your-Sister-Is-Married-to-a-Violent-Criminal Diet. But now it was the Your-Brother-Is-Arrested-for-Shooting-Your-Sister's-Husband Diet. Elizabeth had been struggling to lose weight for most of the semester, and now, ironically, she couldn't force herself to eat. She'd grown so thin over the last two weeks that even her old clothes felt big.

Well, she was here now. She might as well try to eat something. She couldn't afford to waste away.

But Nina was acting strange. She was glancing over Elizabeth's shoulder and seemed unable to look her in the eye.

"Is it okay if I come in?" Elizabeth asked.

"Oh, um, sure." Nina stepped aside.

They sat on her bed and Nina pulled out two croissants. "Is Steven being held in custody? Have you found a lawyer? Is there anything I can do to help?" she asked.

"It's under control for now," Elizabeth said. "Billie is getting Steven a good lawyer. She thinks he'll get out on bail today." She picked at her croissant distractedly.

"That's a relief."

Elizabeth nodded, gazing out the window.

"Is something else worrying you?"

"Like what?" Elizabeth's croissant crumbled into a pile on Nina's bed.

Nina brushed the remains into the palm of her hand and threw them out. "I don't know. I get the feeling there's something you're not telling me."

Elizabeth felt confused. She suddenly realized how alone she was in all this. How she needed to fight this fight by herself. She looked at her friend and found that she had nothing to say.

"I think I know what you're hiding," Nina said, her brown eyes serious. "I know all about Mr. William White."

Nina *knew*?

"Yeah. You can't fool me, Elizabeth Wakefield."

Elizabeth felt the blood pulse in her ears.

"You went home with him after the ball last night, didn't you?"

Elizabeth sagged with relief.

Nina smiled. "So?"

"So what?"

"So what happened?" Nina asked. "Come

on, Elizabeth. You need to get your mind off Steven and Jess for a while and onto something more cheerful."

If only you knew, Elizabeth thought miserably, trying hard to keep her expression even.

"So, tell me, what's under all that mystery?" Nina pressed.

Elizabeth was in no mood for this. But she had to appease her friend. She searched her brain for an answer. It just fell out of her mouth: "Books."

"Books?"

"Um, he likes to read books."

Nina leveled a suspicious eye at Elizabeth. "Last night you read books together?"

"Sort of," Elizabeth replied.

"That's pretty weird," Nina said, looking at her friend intently. "Well, do yourself a favor and don't tell that to anyone else." Nina laughed. "I don't think it would do much for either of your reputations."

"How's Bryan?" Elizabeth asked, eager to change the subject.

"Bryan?" Nina asked.

As if on cue the bathroom door across the hall opened, and out of a cloud of steam walked Bryan himself, shaking out his freshly washed hair. He was wearing one of Nina's more lacy bathrobes. The frilly hem came up to his mid-thigh, and the sleeves were stuck at his elbows.

Nina looked at Bryan with horror, as if she'd totally forgotten he was there. She waved her hands at him, shooing him away. At the sight of Elizabeth, Bryan froze, spun on his heels, and slammed the bathroom door behind him.

Elizabeth felt laughter well up inside her like a spring. She clamped her hand over her mouth to try to keep it from bursting out.

"Elizabeth, I'm *sorry*," Nina said, looking mortified.

"Well, well, well." Elizabeth grinned. "I didn't realize you had company."

Nina was blushing from head to toe.

Elizabeth hugged her friend. "Thank you, Nina."

"Why?" Nina asked, confused.

"This was just what I needed. I can't remember the last time I laughed. It feels like years," Elizabeth said, getting up from the bed. "But obviously, I should be going."

"No, Elizabeth," Nina said, reaching for her. "You stay. Bryan can go."

"Thanks, but I have to be somewhere else. Really. There's something else going on, and—"

"Something *else*?"

"Something big. But I don't think I need to bother you with it now." Elizabeth nodded at the bathroom door. "Just make sure you two watch the news tonight," she called over her shoulder as she headed out the door.

When Isabella Ricci came out of the shower, tugging a comb through her dripping hair, her intelligent gray eyes widened as they caught sight of a surprise waiting for her on her roommate's old bed. The surprise was the old roommate, staring at the blank wall.

Isabella figured Jessica and Mike had had another one of their knock-down-drag-out fights and Jessica was once again threatening to leave him and move back into her old apartment with Isabella.

"There's still room up there for all your old posters," she said calmly, as though continuing a conversation she and Jessica had begun before she went into the shower—as though she'd seen Jessica every day for the last few months, instead of only every now and then after one of her and Mike's blowouts.

Isabella had been sure Jessica would come back eventually. But she'd made a pact with herself not to pressure her in any way. She had always thought it was just a matter of time before her old roommate realized that she'd gotten a little ahead of herself by moving in with Mike McAllery two months into her freshman year of college. Isabella didn't know much about Mike, but what she did know was all bad. It was just going to be a matter of time before Jessica realized that and came home.

"I especially like that life-size one you have of James Dean," Isabella said. "He's so cool."

Jessica didn't answer. She didn't move. She sat perfectly still, as if she were totally numb.

Isabella looked at her for signs of life. This was not the Jessica Wakefield she'd moved in with. That Jessica was fun loving and carefree, interested in every good-looking man she met. If three different guys had asked her out for the weekend, she would have gone out with all of them. She dated hunks, jocks, artsy-fartsy types, and even an occasional dork. Jessica was never that particular. All they had to be was good looking. Jessica called it the shotgun effect: with all those bullets spraying all over the place, she'd have to hit on *something* worthwhile.

"Yeah, like maybe the side of a barn," Isabella used to say to her.

But Jessica hadn't counted on the enigmatic Mike McAllery showing up. It was at the Halloween dance. Some goons were giving Jessica a lot of trouble, and out of nowhere this rebel in a black leather jacket swooped in and decked the guy and swept Jessica away. The rest was history.

"And as you can see," Isabella continued,

"your bed didn't go anywhere. Though I did switch our mattresses. Yours was much fluffier."

Isabella thought that would get a rise out of her. She knew how much Jessica loved big fluffy mattresses. But Jessica just sat there like she was made of stone.

"Oh, and, uh, one other thing. You know I sort of have a boyfriend now. So I was thinking about a system we could use for, uh, you know, privacy. I was thinking of an X on the bulletin board outside the door. What do you think? Jessica? Jessica! Are you listening to me?"

"What was that, Izzy?"

"I said I have a *boyfriend* now."

"Oh. That's what I thought you said. Didn't I know that?"

She is in the clouds, Isabella thought, feeling a tinge of real worry.

Jessica seemed to hesitate before she let the words pass out of her mouth. "Maybe your boyfriend has a good-looking roommate. Maybe we can all double-date or something."

This was getting messy. After all, Jessica was no normal eighteen-year-old anymore. She was *married*.

Okay, keep calm, Isabella said to herself. *Maybe she's finally leaving that goon.*

"Well, um, sure. Maybe we can double with somebody," she said unenthusiastically. "But his roommate might be kind of complicated."

"Why? Who's the lucky guy?"

Isabella looked at Jessica. She seemed to be drifting off somewhere.

"It's Danny, Jess. You knew that. Jess, are you okay?"

"What? Huh? Oh, yeah, I'm okay. Danny. Right. So who's his roommate?"

"Who's his roommate?" Isabella repeated. She knew Jessica knew who Danny's roommate was. She and Mike had had him and Elizabeth over for dinner a few days ago.

"Yeah, who is he?"

"It's Tom," Isabella said. "Tom Watts."

"Tom Watts," Jessica repeated.

"Yeah. Tom *Watts*. Elizabeth's Tom Watts."

"Oh, right. Tom."

"You sure you're okay? Where's Mike?" Isabella asked.

Jessica's eyes brimmed with tears.

"Jess? Jess? What's wrong?"

Jessica turned to her. Her face was splotchy, her eyes were red and puffy, her hands shook. For a second Isabella stopped breathing. This was not any one of the Jessica Wakefields she knew. This Jessica Wakefield was not merely upset but totally helpless, not knowing which way to turn. This Jessica Wakefield was coming apart at the seams.

*   *   *

Tom sat in the deserted WSVU office. The computer hummed softly. He looked around to make sure he was alone. *It always seems like I'm here by myself,* he thought.

Doodling on his desk blotter, he found himself drawing the broken star, then writing over and over next to it: SECRET SOCIETY=WILLIAM WHITE+?

At least Elizabeth believes me now, Tom told himself. *At least she doesn't think I'm the leader of the secret society.*

Magically, as he pictured her in his mind, the real Elizabeth materialized before him as bright morning sunlight filled the room.

"Tom," she said, slightly out of breath.

"You're here early," Tom said. "I didn't expect you until much later."

"I'm so glad to see you," she said in a way that warmed his heart. "You're not going to believe who was waiting in my room for me when you left."

"Let me guess."

"He and Celine had been—how can I put this delicately—"

Tom shook his head. "Well, I can't say I know two people who deserve each other more."

"That's funny," Elizabeth said. "That's just what I said. Then William tried to smooth over what had happened. He actually tried to convince me that he wasn't part of the secret society at all."

"That's just like him," Tom said.

Even in the days when they went to the same parties and social functions, Tom hadn't liked William. As self-absorbed and arrogant as he himself had been then, Tom had never lost sight of how much more self-centered William was. He had never trusted him. William was too smooth, too perfect. His smile gave nothing away—and that had always made Tom nervous. But he had underestimated William. He'd known William was a shady character, but not this shady. Tom was starting to worry. He could deal with shadiness. But William was much more than that.

Elizabeth was gazing off into space.

"You're scheming," Tom said. "I'd know that look anywhere. You're dangerous when you look like that."

"Dangerous enough to take on William White?"

I sure hope so, Tom thought.

Alexandra Rollins banged down the telephone. Again Mark hadn't answered his phone. She'd been trying him all morning. They were supposed to have had breakfast together before his meeting with the dean, but when he didn't show up at the coffee shop, she had gone to his room. He didn't answer the door either. Somehow, she wasn't even surprised. Since he and Todd had come under suspicion in the sports scandal, she and Mark had done almost nothing but argue. She had gotten together with Lauren and come up with a strategy: they'd bombard them with positive thoughts and physical affection. They had to get the guys to stop thinking so negatively.

Lauren seemed more successful. She and Todd still kissed in public, while Mark wouldn't even hold Alexandra's hand. And at least Todd was putting up a fight, protesting his innocence every chance he got, while Mark kept all his feelings to himself. He was getting quieter and quieter. What little he did say about it was laced with phrases like "bad luck" and "going down the tubes" and "I'm doomed."

He had told Alex she couldn't understand what she was going through. And when she reminded him that she was his girlfriend, that he could confide in her, all he said was that nobody could help him. He was all on his own. Once, in a heated moment, he had even said he'd quit SVU before he let them kick him out. When Alex started to cry, he'd kissed her and told her he was only kidding.

But after dialing Mark's phone again and still

getting no answer, Alex wasn't so sure.

She grabbed her jacket and went down to the gym, the one place he was sure to be if he was anywhere. He and Todd probably had gone to shoot baskets after the meeting to let off some steam. She could understand that.

What she couldn't understand was why Todd was shooting baskets by himself at the far end of the field house. There was no one else in sight. The *ping-pa-ping* of Todd's dribbles and the crash of his jumpers against the backboard filled the whole cavernous building with echoes.

She walked across the main court, the one on which she had imagined Mark winning games at the last minute, the one to which professional scouts would flock in droves to see Mark play— the place where she could point and say: "The star of the team is my boyfriend."

She knew Todd had seen her approaching, but he kept on shooting, like he knew why she was there.

"Hey, Todd," Alex said.

"Oh, hey, Alex," Todd said, panting. He turned and took another shot.

"Where's Mark?"

Todd rebounded his own miss and put in an easy layup.

"Todd?"

"I don't know," Todd said.

"Where'd he say he was going?"

"He didn't say he was going anywhere."

It was obvious Todd was covering something up. Alex was starting to get tired of interrogating him. She put her hands on her hips.

"Well, then, Todd, maybe you could tell me what direction he walked in after the meeting?"

Todd caught the ball. He eyed Alex, as if he was deciding whether to say anything. Then he whirled and fired the ball, a high arching jumper that seemed to float above the basket, then missed it completely. Air ball.

"Nice shot," Alex said.

The ball rolled into a corner.

"To tell you the truth," Todd said, "Mark wasn't at the meeting."

Alex felt all the air leave her body.

"He left me a note," Todd continued. "It seems like he took off for a while to be by himself. Maybe he just wants to figure some things out."

"But what did the dean say?"

Todd eyed her again, then obviously decided he might as well finish what he'd started.

"It doesn't look good, Alex," Todd said, then whirled and dribbled away.

You don't want to be with me either, Alex thought. Walking back across the court, she pictured Mark cruising in his Explorer down the coast highway to nowhere . . . music blaring . . .

thinking of nothing . . . all alone . . . designing a new life—without her.

Why do you shut me out?

Out in the air, the warm Southern California sunshine was no comfort. All it did was blind her. Where to go? Theta House? Home? For the first time since she'd been at SVU, she felt completely alone. She had her Theta sisters, but since she'd gotten involved with Mark, she'd practically forgotten about them. Mark was her best friend. She told him everything. It was like he carried everything she was around with him. And now that he was gone, he had taken all of that with him.

And she sure couldn't talk to Elizabeth Wakefield, her best friend from high school, like she once could.

Ex–best friend, she said to herself, taking a turn back to her dorm.

After all, Elizabeth was the cause of the trouble. She and Tom Watts, who had insinuated those lies about the top SVU athletes. It was no coincidence that Elizabeth had directed her report at the basketball team and at its two freshman starters in particular, Mark and Todd.

Alex knew Elizabeth had been crushed when Todd dumped her for Lauren. But Alex had no idea Elizabeth was so vindictive. She never would have thought the Elizabeth she once knew could be so coldhearted. Revenge against Todd—maybe. But this way? By totally ruining his life?

What about Mark? He was just an innocent bystander caught in the cross fire. Why did Elizabeth have to make them all pay for her own misery?

Maybe you were never the friend I thought you were, Alex told the Elizabeth in her head.

Chapter Five

"Okay," Elizabeth said. She had a notepad on her knee and a pen at the ready. "From the beginning."

"Do we really have to do this?" Tom asked.

"We only have a few hours to put together our exposé," Elizabeth argued. "If we can use any of your experience with the secret society as evidence, we need to get it all out on the table." She raised her eyes to his.

Tom sighed. Elizabeth wanted to know about his old life, and he wanted to tell her. This wasn't the part of it he wanted to tell her, but it was a place to start. "It all began when I became starting quarterback for the football team," Tom began slowly. "I was sleeping in my dorm one night when someone nudged me awake. I opened my eyes and found myself surrounded by five guys in ski masks. Danny wasn't in his bed. They must have known he'd be out. Or maybe they arranged it. I never knew. I thought it was a nightmare. 'This isn't a nightmare, Watts,' one of them said, like he was reading my mind.

"I got out of bed and asked them who they were, breaking into my room in the middle of the night. You have to understand, Elizabeth"— Tom looked sheepishly at the ground, embarrassed by what he was about to tell her—"that was the other Tom Watts."

"Wildman," Elizabeth said.

"Wildman," Tom repeated. "It was only a couple of years ago, but it feels like a lifetime. Back then I was kind of important on campus. Or I *thought* I was—"

"Yeah, yeah, I know," Elizabeth said, leaning forward eagerly. "BMOC Tom 'Wildman' Watts. The big stud. So go on."

"So, I thought I should be treated with, you know—"

"A little respect?"

"Yeah, that's it. Anyway," Tom continued, "these clowns got me out of bed and got me to agree to being blindfolded—I don't know why I agreed—and they took me somewhere in their car. It felt like we were driving for hours. When we stopped, they led me down to a beach. I could hear the surf and feel sand under my feet. They took my blindfold off. In front of me was a group of about twenty guys. They all had on ski masks and capes, and they were holding torches. Their capes had these insignias—"

"The broken star," Elizabeth said excitedly. To her, all this was like putting together the pieces of a jigsaw puzzle. But to Tom, it was much more than that.

"Above the broken star was written F-O-G," he went on grimly.

"Fog?"

"The Fraternal Order of the Gallows."

"How creepy."

"You have no idea the power these guys have," Tom continued. "If I didn't join them at the beach that night, they told me I'd never start at quarterback for SVU again, I'd never amount to anything."

"And that's why you did it?" Elizabeth asked breathlessly.

Tom thought for a moment and shook his head. "Part of it, maybe. Mostly I did it because I was an arrogant piece of crap and I wasn't smart enough to know any better."

He studied Elizabeth's face and found so much compassion there he decided to go on. He had to admit it felt too good to be getting all this off his chest. Finally, to be telling someone the truth. A someone who just happened to be a beautiful woman he'd fallen head over heels in love with.

"They are powerful, though. The list of members of the secret society is like a *Who's Who* of American history. When members graduate from college, they're set for life. They can work anywhere. Washington, Paris, London . . ."

"But I don't get it," Elizabeth said. "What *is* the secret society, exactly?"

"I'm not sure what it *does*. I never got too involved. But it seemed to be in the business of protecting itself. Everything the society did seemed connected to making its members more and more powerful."

"That doesn't seem like a very *intelligent* reason for a club, if you ask me," Elizabeth said.

"Intelligence didn't have much to do with it." Tom cringed. "In fact, any *intelligent* person would have seen how ridiculous the whole thing was. Any *intelligent* person would have refused to join it."

Elizabeth put her hand on Tom's shoulder. "You're so hard on yourself. They practically forced you into it."

Oh, sweet Elizabeth, Tom thought, gazing adoringly into her eyes, *if only you knew how I was then*.

"Well, they did and they didn't," Tom confessed. "I mean, maybe at the beach that night, just maybe I got swept up by the whole thing. I mean, they wanted *me*, Tom Watts, to be part of *them*. In a strange way, even though I didn't know what *them* was, it felt kind of good."

"Did you know how violent they were then?" Elizabeth asked, sitting on the edge of her seat. "Did you know they were racists?"

"I didn't know that concretely," Tom said thoughtfully. "When I began to realize what was going on, I started to back out, then . . . well, then other things happened in my life and I dropped out completely." Tom was looking down at his hands when he finished.

"Are the society members just full of hate?" Elizabeth asked. "Is that why they want to hurt people?"

"That's not the point exactly, although a lot of them are. And when they get together, the mob mentality takes over and the hatred grows. But in the beginning violence was a last resort in order to protect themselves. Now they seem to want to blot out anyone who's not just like they are. Like Nina and Bryan, for instance, who look different than they do. Bryan is part of a movement to make SVU more aware of minority rights and issues. He and Nina were easy targets."

"Well, now FOG, or whatever you want to

105

call them, has made *itself* a target," Elizabeth stated.

"Okay, superwoman. But we're going to have to stick together. You're a target now because William White knows you know. I'm obviously a target, too. I've done the unthinkable—I've told an outsider about the society. And now we're going to tell the world. So please, please be careful."

The boulevards of Paris were flying by. The thick crowd of spectators pressing in on both sides of the cobblestone streets was a blur. Winston Egbert's legs worked mechanically, furiously, propelling him like pistons in a V-8 engine past one bicyclist after another. The Frenchmen and their pretty mademoiselles were going wild. "Viva la Américain!" they were crying, waving little American flags. A total unknown, American Winston Egbert, had emerged out of the back of the pack and appeared beside the leaders of the Tour de France just as they were leaving the French Alps. Today was the race's last leg, the last day, the last mile. Up ahead, exploding out of the ground, was the Arc de Triomphe. Winston's legs redoubled their effort. His eyes went out of focus. At the finish line was a slender, intelligent, gorgeous woman named Denise Waters who stood in the middle of the Champs Élysées. He put her in his crosshairs, bit his lip, and leaned into the wind . . .

"Winston? Yo, Winston!"

Danny Wyatt was leaning toward Winston from the neighboring stationary bike at the campus gym. "Win! Anybody home?"

Winston stopped cycling and felt his face flush redder than it already was. "Danny, hi." He was struggling for breath. His face was streaked with sweat. "Sorry about that. I was just . . . uh . . . thinking . . ."

"About Denise Waters," Danny finished.

Winston gave him a lopsided smile. "Was it that obvious?"

"You two looked like you were having an incredible time last night," Danny said.

Winston panted. "We were. It was more than incredible."

"So why do you look so worried?" Danny asked.

"Well, I just keep thinking of Denise lying on top of my blankets," Winston said dreamily.

"Uh-huh. I get it. She left you hanging," Danny concluded, chuckling.

"On *top* of the blankets is the real problem here," Winston went on philosophically. He looked at Danny with the wide-open eyes of an innocent, waiting for his instructions. "Now what?"

107

"You're getting greedy, aren't you?"

"Not greedy. Logical," Winston insisted. "It only makes sense. First we study together. We laugh and joke together. We go to the movies and play pool together. She helps me wash my car and we trade CDs—"

"She washed your car?" Danny cried in mock horror. "This really might be love."

"*She* asked me to the ball. *She* kissed me first."

"So?"

"Can't you see, Danny? It's been a perfectly logical progression. Like a pyramid."

"You sound like a math geek."

Winston stared off into space. His whole future lay before him. A white palatial home, children frolicking on the lawn, luscious Denise every night, every morning . . .

"It's like we're destined for each other," he said dreamily. "You're lost, buddy," Danny said.

"What I don't understand," Winston went on, as though Danny hadn't said anything, "is how one of the most beautiful, intelligent, and sought-after women on this campus would go for me."

"Don't overestimate yourself or anything," Danny said sarcastically.

"I mean, I'm so . . . so . . ."

"Goofy?"

"Yeah . . . I mean, *no*." Winston looked at Danny with exasperation written all over his face. "I'm just . . ."

"Not her type?" Danny suggested. Talking to Winston sometimes was like doing Mad Libs; all you had to do was fill in the blanks. "Look, Winston, love is like that. There's no explaining it. It's the mistakes, the things you never would have guessed that sometimes work out the best. Look at me. Who ever would have thought Isabella Ricci would give me the time of day? She had a crush on Tom since the first day of school."

Winston seemed to deflate. The Tour de France champion vanished. "I guess so."

"Don't look at it so closely, Win. You'll chase it away."

Winston thought for a minute. "But didn't Socrates or somebody say, 'An unexamined life is not worth living'?"

"Well, Socrates didn't have a shot at Denise Waters."

Winston sagged lower. "You're right."

"What's the problem? Why look so down? Maybe you forgot. Let me spell it out for you: You-got-the-girl."

The light returned to Winston's eyes. "I got her," he said, pepping himself up. "I got her. I got her." It was like a dream. "And now that I've got her—"

Danny smiled expectantly. "And now that you've got her," he egged him on.

"And now that I've got her . . . *what?*"

Danny nudged him with his elbow and winked. "You're the one who believes in logical progression."

Winston just stared at him, aghast. It suddenly all seemed terribly wrong. It was one thing to kiss Denise and hold her in his arms. It was another to even contemplate . . . what came next. On the one hand, he'd been lusting after her for what seemed like ages. But on the other, she was like a sister to him.

"Don't look at me like you don't know what I'm talking about," Danny said.

Winston blushed.

"Win," Danny said, throwing his towel over Winston's head, "take it from me: you *are* goofy."

Todd leaned against a tree outside the WSVU station. He'd told himself he was just going for a walk. That was what he said when he left the gym right after he saw Alex and went straight to Dickenson Hall and up to Elizabeth's room.

That was what he said when he heard

Celine's voice through the door arguing with some uptight, pseudo-sophisticated guy and headed over to the library to check carrel 2 in the reading room, Elizabeth's favorite carrel.

And that's what he said when he didn't find her there and made a beeline for the television station. Just a stroll on this beautiful day. And if he *happened* to run into Elizabeth, well, accidents did happen . . .

But as Elizabeth emerged from the doorway, squinting into the dazzling sun, Todd suddenly got cold feet. He glanced around him. He was standing between two trees. There was nothing else around. There was nowhere to hide, unless he just stood still and hoped Elizabeth mistook him for a tree. After all, he had the height.

But as Elizabeth's face tilted forward in a confused smile, he realized he might have had the height, but not the leaves.

She marched purposefully toward him. He couldn't help the feelings that flooded his mind. The memories.

She was dressed in faded jeans and a simple, long-sleeved pink T-shirt, but she looked staggeringly beautiful to him. Her long pale hair hung loose around her shoulders, and a backpack was slung over one shoulder.

111

At the beginning of the semester Elizabeth had seemed slightly heavy and awkward, uncomfortable with herself. She had been so depressed then that he'd decided college just didn't agree with her.

Clearly he'd been wrong. Because now the sight of her took his breath away.

Just smile and say hello, he advised himself. *Smile, say hello, and say you have someplace to be . . .*

"Liz!" Todd exclaimed with feigned surprise.

Elizabeth smiled awkwardly. "Hi, Todd. Uh, what are you doing here?"

"I was just walking over to . . . over to the . . . cafeteria."

Elizabeth looked around at the empty expanse surrounding the station. "Oh," she said, looking at him with disbelief. "Really."

Todd shifted from one foot to the other. "Well, no, Liz. Not really. Actually, I was sort of hoping I might run into you." An expression of gloom passed over his face.

"Are you okay, Todd?"

"I had that meeting with the dean this morning."

Elizabeth jammed her hands in her pockets. Her face went pink in embarrassment.

He'd already told her he'd stopped blaming her for reporting the athletics exposé that had

112

gotten him into this mess. He'd told her he knew she wasn't the kind of person to try to get revenge. But still, the whole issue left a feeling of awkwardness between them. Awkwardness even beyond the fact that they had been so much in love before, that he'd broken her heart.

"What did he say?" Elizabeth asked.

"That's what I came to talk to you about. It looks like Mark has decided it's all over. He wasn't even there this morning. He took off. I don't know where. He left me a note, though. I don't think he's coming back."

Elizabeth opened her mouth, but it was obvious she was at a loss for words. She gazed over his shoulder. "Poor Alex," she said softly.

"Don't blame yourself for that, Elizabeth. It's his decision." Todd paused. "But it's not mine." He thought hard for his words. He wanted to be careful. He didn't want to ask for too much. The only problem was he *did* want something.

"The dean didn't say for sure what was going to happen," Todd said. "But he hinted around at it. He just said I should start looking after myself, as if the school wouldn't anymore."

"But that's not fair!" Elizabeth protested. "It's the administration's responsibility—"

"So I want to do that now," Todd said quietly, cutting her off. "I want to start looking after myself. I'm going out of my mind, worrying. Lauren's no help. She's just worried about herself. I know I'm innocent. But I need a defense, and I thought . . . well—"

"You want me to help," Elizabeth finished the thought. She was always so good at that. All through their relationship, she seemed to sense exactly what was on his mind.

"Todd, you didn't do anything wrong," she stated flatly. "It would be my responsibility to help. Tom and I—"

Todd winced and stopped hearing. The mention of Tom Watts pained him. He didn't want Tom Watts to help him.

Suddenly he grabbed both her hands in his and peered into her eyes.

"I want you—" Todd blurted, his voice deep with emotion. But Elizabeth's fingers were limp. Her face had a surprised, stricken look. "—to help me," he said quickly.

He shook his head. Standing in front of Elizabeth with her hands in his transported him back in time to the days when they were the perfect couple, the couple who would always last, whose wedding would be the first in their group of friends.

Then Todd had met Lauren. She was flashy, risky. She wore sexy clothes and expensive perfume. On the surface she seemed more fun than Elizabeth, more what he wanted.

"I was wrong, Elizabeth," Todd said, gripping her hands tighter. "I—I—"

"You can count on my help," Elizabeth said, almost coldly.

Just then the door to the station burst open again. Tom hesitated when he spotted them, then approached, his face set with determination.

Todd dropped Elizabeth's hands and took a step back.

"Tom," Elizabeth said. "Todd was just telling me about his meeting with the dean."

Tom and Todd eyed each other suspiciously.

"They're turning him and Mark into scapegoats," Elizabeth went on.

"Look, I've got to go," Todd said suddenly, pretending to glance at his watch. "Thanks for your time, Liz. Good to see you, Watts. Bye."

Todd gave a vague wave as he hurried off across the ball fields. He didn't look back.

"That was weird," Elizabeth said to Tom as she watched Todd hustle away across the quad. "We were in the middle of a conversation."

"It looks like Todd has more on his mind than basketball," Tom said, suddenly looking worried.

"I don't know," Elizabeth said. "I used to know him so well. I used to be able to guess what he was thinking just by looking at him. But I don't know anymore. It's like he's a total stranger."

"Well, I *do* know."

"So what is it, Tom?" Elizabeth knew that sounded more like a challenge than a question.

Tom flushed and looked down at the sidewalk, shifting his feet. Elizabeth saw how uncomfortable she had just made him. She reached for his hand.

"I'm sorry—"

"Don't be," Tom snapped. "It was none of my business. I should have just kept my mouth shut."

"No, Tom," Elizabeth said, squeezing his fingers. "It *is* your business. I *want* it to be."

Elizabeth realized that was as close as she'd ever come to an open declaration of her feelings for Tom. And like everything else that had to do with him, what she said or felt just came out of her mouth, just fell out like it was the most natural thing in the world.

"Okay, Elizabeth," Tom said, his tone very businesslike now as he obviously tried to change the subject. "I've rearranged the station's schedule so that the secret society story will air tomorrow night. You know what that means."

Elizabeth nodded.

116

"Be prepared for some backlash," Tom said.

Elizabeth suddenly looked a little nervous. "I'll be okay."

"Just remember that I'm right behind you."

I'd sort of rather have you beside me, Elizabeth thought.

They started walking back toward Elizabeth's dorm.

"So what's happening with your brother?" Tom asked.

Elizabeth's face fell. She would have been glad for a distraction, for the chance to think about something—anything—other than her brother and sister and Mike McAllery. *But family always hovers around you,* she thought. *When you can't see it, you can feel it.*

"Right now Steven's home with Billie," Elizabeth told Tom. "He's out on bail until the trial begins." She studied her hands. "His lawyers are worried he'll be convicted," she said quietly. "That he'll have to serve time. They're trying to work out a deal, but the district attorney is coming up for reelection in a few months, and he's playing hardball. He's not giving an inch. He's cracking down on everything, especially on SVU students. He says college kids think they're above the law, but that they have to accept the consequences of their actions just like everybody else."

They stopped in front of Elizabeth's dorm.

"I can't even think about what we'll do if he's convicted," she said wearily, tears welling in her eyes.

"God, it's hard to take," Tom said.

Elizabeth searched Tom's eyes. "I still have faith in the court. Everyone in the world knows it was an accident. I feel sorry for Mike, but he started it. I truly believe everything will come out the way it should."

"Forever the optimist," Tom said, his eyes shining.

"It's just that I've always thought that when you believe in something hard enough, and if you've done everything you can, you'll get what you deserve."

"Everything?" Tom said quietly. Their eyes met for a long, powerful moment.

Elizabeth felt her heart pounding as Tom leaned forward slightly. She was drawn closer, as if the air between them had taken on a magnetic current. Tom's lips were so close Elizabeth could feel his breath . . .

Suddenly the door to the dorm crashed open. It scared her as though it were an explosion. Elizabeth and Tom were wedged apart. Even in the shadow, the flash of honey hair was unmistakable.

"Well, well, well," Celine drawled, turning up the heat on her Southern accent. "If it isn't Romeo and Juliet."

Elizabeth and Tom whirled around. The sight of Celine's blinding grin would have been bad enough. But behind her was something that made Elizabeth's blood run cold: William White, his hair slicked back, his black tailored suit tapered to a dagger point, his eyes red with rage.

Chapter Six

Jessica had no memory of falling asleep. Even as she gradually regained consciousness, she wondered where she was. She could tell from the sounds and the smells that she was someplace familiar, but someplace she thought she'd never be again. She opened one eye, then the other. It was just as she'd feared: Mike's apartment.

After seeing Isabella, she'd gone back to pick up the rest of her stuff. She'd sat down on the bed to change her shoes. She had lain back, suddenly overcome with sadness. That was the last thing she remembered. She must have just put her head down on the pillow and fallen asleep. What time was it? She turned her head to the glowing green numbers of the clock radio. Seven o'clock! It felt creepy to be here. The sheets smelled like Mike. He seemed so far away, yet the ache behind her ribs didn't. As much as she would have liked, she couldn't pretend it away. Staring at the bed, she longed for only one thing: Mike the way he used to be, dashing, brave, overflowing with love for her.

She had started to quickly gather her things when the phone rang. She ignored it. It might be a reporter who had found out the identity of the victim, and she sure didn't want her name caught up in all this. Then again, it could be Billie with news about Steven's case, or Elizabeth, or her parents. Her parents!

She ran to the phone, praying it was her mother or father.

"Hello!" she yelled, out of breath.

"Is this Jessica?"

It *was* an older woman's voice. But not her mother's.

Jessica froze.

"Hello, is anybody there?" The woman spoke slowly, with the cold, careful accent of the very well educated—or the very rich. Every syllable enunciated. Every vowel stressed.

"Yes, this is Jessica," she said hesitantly. "Who's this?"

"We never met. I suppose Michael didn't mention me. You probably don't even know he has a mother. But I *am* his mother, you see. And I am at the hospital. They called me last night."

Jessica was stunned. Everything Mike had told her about his mother flooded her brain. He had never said much at one time. He'd doled out the story piece by piece, when something he'd seen or heard reminded him of his childhood. All together, the information he had let out didn't make much more than a rough sketch. What she knew was that Mike had grown up in a very wealthy oil family. Mr. McAllery was the chairman of an offshore drilling company. Mrs. McAllery was cold and distant. Mike had really been brought up by a nanny. Then, when Mike was fourteen, Mrs. McAllery just walked out without an explanation. Since then she'd written twice a year: cards on Christmas and Mike's birthday. The cards never said anything, really. Just the regular old Hallmark cards, signed *Love, Mother.* "She let Hallmark say it for her," Mike always said sarcastically. Every year on his birthday it was the same gift: a shirt box from Ralph Lauren. And every year he'd take it down to the Salvation Army and donate the unopened box to charity.

Jessica knew what it meant for his mother to fly in to see him, for the two of them to be together after all these years.

"Jessica," Mrs. McAllery said, "I'm sitting with Mike. Don't worry, I know everything. I don't blame you, dear. Mike made sure to tell everyone that all this was his fault, that you were innocent."

"You know Mike had a gun."

Mrs. McAllery said nothing. The silence vibrated with resentment and bad history. But still, Jessica thought his mother needed to hear this. She needed to know about her son. "Mike isn't well. He's dangerous," Jessica continued.

"I know about the gun, Jessica," Mrs. McAllery answered coolly. "But the only thing that matters now is for Mike to live. He's been in and out of consciousness. The doctors . . ." Mrs. McAllery trailed off. If Jessica hadn't known better, she would have thought Mike's mother was actually crying.

"I'm sorry to have to tell you this," Mrs. McAllery went on. "The doctors have given him a fifty-fifty chance. And even if he lives, they're not sure he'll ever walk again."

Jessica swallowed hard.

"He keeps asking for you, Jessica," Mrs. McAllery said. "He's been asking for you all day. It's all he wants, just to see you again."

The voice turned colder. "I've never seen Mike feel this way about anybody. You must be quite beautiful."

Jessica had no reply. She had the feeling she was being manipulated.

"The doctors told me that sometimes a loved

one's presence can pull a critical patient through," Mrs. McAllery continued, her voice breaking slightly. "Just a moment of happiness— it can have an effect like a drug. For someone on the edge . . . like Mike . . . sometimes it's all that it takes—"

Jessica listened in disbelief. Now she was sure. Mrs. McAllery *was* crying. Now tears flooded her eyes, too. But she couldn't let herself lose control now. She had to be strong. She'd made her decision. She was going to start all over. Make herself a new life.

"I'll do my best to see him," Jessica said.

"Will you? Tonight? Mike will be so happy."

Jessica knew she'd say anything just to get off the phone. Part of her felt that Mike and his mother deserved each other. But there was still this other part of her that felt the tug of obligation.

"I have to go now," Jessica said curtly.

"Then you *will* come tonight," Mrs. McAllery insisted with that cold authority Mike had described. "I can tell my son that?"

"No, don't tell Mike anything," Jessica replied. "I'll try to come."

But when the telephone hit the cradle, she knew she never would.

This is going to be really good, Celine said to herself.

She and William and Elizabeth and Tom were facing one another in the entrance to Dickenson Hall. Both couples were trying to get through, but neither was willing to give ground. William blocked the path, his black coat spread behind him like a cape, his pale, chiseled face twisted in a grin.

Tom managed to get Elizabeth safely behind him and stepped up toward William. Physically, it would have been no match, Celine thought. Tom was taller and more powerful than William. But William's power was never his physical strength. It was his raw nerve, his cleverness.

"You wouldn't touch me, Watts," William said. "You couldn't."

"Couldn't I?" Tom said, and shoved William into the glass door.

The door shuddered and threatened to shatter.

"Tom!" Elizabeth cried. "We don't need to do this. Please?"

"Miss Holier-Than-Thou," Celine said. "Always falling on the side of justice for all."

"I think you two should just leave," Elizabeth said to Tom and William. "Go home and take cold showers, both of you." She started for the door. "Please, Tom. You wouldn't want to jeopardize our case."

"You wouldn't want to jeopardize the little itty-bitty case, Tommy," Celine mocked.

126

Righteous performances like these always burned Celine up. Nobody could be as right all the time as Elizabeth pretended to be. The girl was nothing but a hypocrite, as far as Celine was concerned.

Elizabeth closed her eyes as if she was about to scream. "Just go home! Everybody!" she cried.

"Not until I talk to you . . . *alone*, Elizabeth," William said, grabbing her arm.

"It's all over, William. Let go of her," Tom said, grabbing Elizabeth's other arm.

I hope they pull her apart and her stuffing falls out, Celine thought.

Elizabeth wrenched her arms free and pushed herself through the door.

"This is your last warning, Elizabeth," William commanded her, pointing an ominous finger. "Drop this nonsense before it's too late."

Elizabeth settled her gaze on his white-blue eyes. "Too late for what, William?"

"You're the investigative reporter," William taunted. "I'll leave it to you to find out. But at this rate you won't have to wait too long, or look too hard."

"Is that a threat?" Elizabeth asked. "Because if it is, that was very careless. I have a witness," she said, gesturing to Tom.

"Watts? You think he's innocent? When are you going to believe me? He's as deep into this as anyone else."

"It's too late, White," Tom said. "I told her everything. The initiation ceremonies. Everything. We know it was you who attacked Nina Harper and Bryan Nelson. We don't only know it. We can prove it."

"You're bluffing!"

"Am I?" Tom said, folding his arms.

"Watts, when this is all over, the marshals are going to be waiting at your room to slap you with a nice fat libel suit."

"Not unless you can sue me from inside a six-by-six cell. You're through at SVU," Tom said, meeting William's gaze. "You're through."

William whirled and vanished into the dark. Tom followed close behind. Their taunts echoed through the courtyard of Dickenson Hall.

Celine turned to Elizabeth. "You sure have those boys wound up," she cooed.

Elizabeth scowled at her roommate. "Don't talk to me, Celine. Don't even look at me." She turned and headed for the stairs.

"What did Tom mean about it being too late?" Celine called to her.

Elizabeth stopped. "I'm making my TV debut tomorrow night," she said. "Be sure to watch. I'm sure you'll find it interesting."

Elizabeth turned her back and took the stairs two at a time.

Not if I can help it, Celine thought. She marched to the pay phone in the commons room and dialed William's number.

"We need to talk," she said into the answering machine. "It's worse than we thought. It's no bluff."

As Jessica walked down the hallway of Mike's apartment building with another box of her belongings in her arms, she heard a familiar voice call her name. It was a voice she had known all her life, a voice she grew up with. But hearing it now, she thought it was the sweetest, freshest voice she'd ever heard. It was Steven's.

"Jess!"

Jessica dropped the box, whirled around, and sprinted down the hall to her brother.

"Whoa, girl," Steven said as Jessica ran into his arms.

She gave him a long hug. "You smell awful," she said when she pulled away.

"Well, they don't exactly hand out deodorant and soap in the county jail," Steven said with a laugh.

Jessica studied her brother's face. "And you *look* worse!"

Billie appeared behind them, laughing with

129

relief. "He looks like an ex-con," she said. "I sort of like it. You know, that unshaven, rough-and-tumble kind of look." She winked at Jessica.

Suddenly Steven sobered and seemed to sag. "Jessica." It sounded like a plea. "I'm so—" He took his sister into his arms again. "I'm sorry, I'm sorry, I'm so sorry. I don't know how it happened. I never meant to hurt him."

"It wasn't your fault," Jessica said, hugging him tighter. Then Steven stood back and held her at arm's length. "I know I said all those things about Mike. I know I said I'd like to kill him. But I never, ever meant it like that—"

"I know, Steven. There were times when he didn't come home and I promised that if he wasn't dead, I was going to kill him, too. No one's saying it's your fault."

"Except the district attorney."

"Don't worry about him," Billie said. "The charges won't stick. I've been talking to lawyers all day. After the indictment tomorrow, you'll be free and clear. That's what the lawyers said."

"What's happened to us?" Steven said, shaking his head. Jessica could see that his eyes glistened with tears.

Jessica gazed off into space, replaying in her brain the shooting for the millionth time. She flinched as she heard the gunshot again. She saw her brother and Mike tumble to the floor . . . all that blood . . . Mike's face as white as a ghost's.

"It's okay," she said distractedly, trying to wipe the vision from her mind. "I know you were only trying to protect me. I'm just glad it wasn't—"

Billie walked up and put her arms around both of them. "Go ahead, Jess. It's okay to say it."

"I'm just glad it wasn't you who was shot," Jessica said, her voice trembling.

"Jess, I need you to testify on my behalf," Steven said.

"Of course," said Jessica.

She saw Billie and Steven exchange a worried look.

"It will mean testifying against your own husband," Billie reminded her.

"I understand," Jessica said without hesitating.

Again her mind wandered to Mike. It was like looking at a movie. For every scene of good times she made sure to throw in one of the bad. The first time they made love; the unmistakable scent of another woman in his hair. Their romantic elopement in Las Vegas; the sound of his drunken slur. She felt herself hardening toward Mike as the minutes went by.

"It won't be a problem," Jessica said. "I'll tell it just like it happened. I would do anything to keep you out of jail, Steven."

As Jessica walked back to the apartment for

another load of her stuff—wishing, for the first time, that she didn't have such a big wardrobe—she knew that she couldn't go to the hospital. She wanted to be done with Mike. All she wanted, all she wanted at that very minute, was to have her normal college life back again. And this time she wouldn't let anything take it away.

Todd slumped over his desk, poring over an album brimming with photos of high school, mostly ones of him and Elizabeth. He wasn't even supposed to have any of these pictures left. When he and Lauren had first started going out, she'd made him promise to throw out the entire album. He had happily agreed.

He had brought the pictures to the incinerator in the basement and opened the door. The intense heat leapt out at him. He had stared into the leaping and hissing flames, then offered them the album. The plastic cover began to singe and smoke. But something made him reach in and pull it back out before it was too late. He carried the album back upstairs and shoved it under some papers in a drawer. He wasn't sure why, exactly. He hadn't even thought much about it. Until now.

Now he knew why.

He handled the pages delicately, careful not to tear the plastic where it was singed. He

132

stared at a picture of him and Elizabeth, holding each other on a wide, sunny beach. It was junior year, not long after they'd first started going out. They looked so happy together, so madly in love.

He flipped to the back of the album, to the most recent pictures. There was one from their last night at home in Sweet Valley. Elizabeth looked so beautiful, leaning on his car in front of the Box Tree Café, laughing.

Todd smiled at the photograph. An ironic, crooked smile. The memory seemed like a bad joke. He had ended the perfect relationship.

And now there was Lauren . . . and Tom. Todd knew Lauren wasn't right for him. He'd had that sinking feeling after the thrill of their first week together tarnished into a routine. She had only proved the point these last few weeks, during the sports scandal. When he needed her most, she just wasn't there.

But Elizabeth and Tom he wasn't as sure about. He couldn't tell what Elizabeth's relationship to Tom was. Todd had been watching them for a while now. Sometimes Elizabeth seemed to really care about Tom, to look at him with that sparkle in her eye, as if he was her boyfriend or at least a good friend. Then two nights ago she had gone to the charity ball with that William White creep. But just today, at the

WSVU station, Elizabeth and Tom had seemed to be hanging around together like an old couple. They had looked so comfortable together. Todd just couldn't figure them out.

Maybe this is the way things are supposed to be, he thought. *We've grown up over the past months. Now it's time to get back together. Maybe I just needed a big shake-up to realize how much I love Elizabeth.*

Behind him, the door opened.

"Hello?" he called out.

There was no answer. And when he turned in his chair, he saw Lauren.

Todd quickly covered the photo album with some class notes. "Don't you know how to knock?" he asked peevishly.

"I didn't think I had to," Lauren replied, raising her eyebrows. "You never said I had to before."

Her gaze landed on the desk. Todd had managed to conceal the entire album except one crisp corner. She blinked, seeming numb with surprise.

"Uh, sorry," Todd stammered. "I'm kind of out of it, with . . . you know . . . I—I—"

"You jerk!" Lauren shrieked.

"I was just flipping through some old team pictures," Todd said feebly.

"You were going to get rid of that stuff—but

134

you couldn't!" Lauren hid her face. "You've been in love with her this whole time." She slumped down on the bed and began to cry.

Todd said nothing. What could he say? She was right.

Lauren looked up, her face streaked with black mascara, obviously hoping he would say something, anything.

Todd knew he could say one soothing thing and reassure her. It would be so easy. He wouldn't even have to mean it. She'd believe anything. She always had. He knew that if he just opened his mouth, he could have her back and it would be like it was before.

But his jaw wouldn't move. That did it. That was the answer: he didn't want her.

As if she read his thoughts, Lauren got to her feet, took two steps to where Todd was sitting, and slapped him hard once across his cheek. Then she stormed out, leaving the door wide open behind her.

Jessica let the phone ring what felt like a thousand times before she picked up.

"Jess?"

"Thank God it's you, Liz," Jessica said, and sank onto the couch.

"Who else were you expecting?"

"Mike's mother called."

"Mike's mother! I thought you said he didn't have a mother."

Jessica sighed. "Well, he didn't, really. I mean, of course he had one. Everybody has a mother. But his ran out on him and his father when he was fourteen. Now she's back. She's at the hospital. I promised her I'd go see Mike."

Elizabeth was silent. Jessica knew what that meant. It meant that she wanted Jessica to go, too, but wanted her to reach that conclusion by herself. It was an old trick of Elizabeth's—lead Jessica to an answer, then let her think she'd found it herself.

"I know what you're thinking, Liz," Jessica said.

"Really? What?" Elizabeth answered innocently.

Jessica didn't reply.

"Come on, Jess. You already know what I think. But what I think doesn't matter. We both know that you won't go until you're ready, so what's the point in me badgering you?"

"You're right," Jessica said. "There is no point." But she began to feel herself caving in. *Elizabeth is always right,* a little voice whispered in Jessica's ear. *You've got to go see him. It's your responsibility.*

Elizabeth paused. "That's actually not why I'm calling. What I wanted to know is if I can

136

offer you a place to stay tonight. I know you don't want to stay there. And after all, we Wakefields have to stick together."

"Thanks, Liz. Really. But I have to pick myself up. I told Isabella I was moving back in with her. I've got to start looking out for myself."

Jessica thought she heard her twin breathe a sigh of relief. "That's great, Jess. I'm really glad you're going back to the dorm. That's a great first step. But if you change your mind, you're always welcome. You can have Celine's bed."

"What about the creature? Where will she sleep?"

"I have this sneaking suspicion she won't be staying here tonight."

"That's unusual," Jessica replied.

"That's not the only unusual thing going on," Elizabeth said. "I have a lot to tell you. But it can wait until tomorrow. You have enough on your mind. Good night, Jess."

"Night, Elizabeth."

Jessica put down the phone and finished packing her things. Just as she was about to leave the apartment for what she hoped was the last time, the phone rang again. She assumed Elizabeth had forgotten to tell her something. She picked it up.

"Hello?"

"Jessica, darling."

Jessica said nothing. It was Mrs. McAllery.

"Please, Jessica. Mike calls for you every conscious moment."

Jessica could hear a gravelly coughing in the background. It was Mike—her *husband*, she reminded herself. She thought she heard his voice, a hoarse whisper. "Jess . . . please," was all she could make out.

Jessica could feel her heart breaking. She felt her concern for Mike well up deep inside her, although she tried to keep it down. It was an instinct.

"Please . . . Jess," Mike groaned.

It suddenly struck Jessica that her feelings for Mike were unavoidable, that despite all his problems, and the problems he caused her, all he ever wanted was to be her husband.

And now he might pull through, she thought. *If I'm the only one who can save him . . .*

"Mrs. McAllery," Jessica said with conviction, "I'm on my way."

Jessica slammed down the phone, rushed out the door, and ran down to the parking lot to her car.

Elizabeth's slumber was deep, her dream vivid. Like one of those crisp, cool days when there isn't a cloud in the sky and everything seems sharp and alive and breathing with light.

Everything in the dream moved slowly and tranquilly, like a silent movie. Even the bright green waves tumbling one after the other onto the beach.

She and Tom were standing ankle deep in the sand. Down the shore on the left a meeting of the secret society was going on, but she and Tom were too far away to see or hear them; down the beach on the right stood a group consisting of Elizabeth's family—her parents, Jessica, Steven—Billie, and even Mike McAllery lying on a stretcher hooked up to an I.V. But they also were too far away to care about. All her problems were far away.

Elizabeth's eyes were fixed solely on Tom. They were facing each other, holding hands. But Elizabeth saw all thoughts of the secret society story, or any story but their own, drain from his bottomless eyes. She had always thought she'd be able to fall headlong into those eyes if only she'd been given the chance. And now here it was, her face only inches from his, and nothing around them but stretches of white sand and an endless ocean of cool green water for thousands of miles.

Tom broke the silence. "I never thought I'd find someone as smart as you," he whispered. "Or as beautiful."

Elizabeth looked so hard into his eyes she

thought she'd shatter them, like a pebble falling into the glassy surface of a pond. All thoughts of the secret society story left her. What she wanted now was a simple yes or no answer: *Do you love me?*

Suddenly Tom's mouth opened. Elizabeth couldn't believe what she heard.

"I'm too afraid to try," Tom whispered.

That was her favorite line from the love poem slipped under her door a few weeks ago. She had hoped Tom was the author, but William White had taken credit for it.

She raised her hand and put a finger to Tom's lips. She didn't need to hear another word: she'd already committed the whole poem to memory. Her heart skipped a beat. She felt giddy and scared all at once. But a good scared. An excited scared. As though her life was finally moving forward. Finally—at last!—she felt alive again. She felt the bittersweet memory of Todd, and the distinctly sour recollection of William White, move off like two ghosts.

Tom leaned toward her. Elizabeth closed her eyes. She felt his lips touch hers. They were soft, the most tender lips in the world. . . .

Elizabeth woke with a start. She felt herself smiling, although there was no beach, only her darkened dorm room.

She could see the lump that was Celine in her bed. That surprised her. She really hadn't thought

Celine would have the guts to come back after what had happened with Tom and William. For a second she thought something was strange. She couldn't hear a faint snoring. Usually Celine purred in her sleep like she did when she was awake. But now there was nothing but silence, as though Celine wasn't asleep but awake, quiet and watchful.

Still, what a dream! Elizabeth had never had one like it before. It was so real, it wasn't like a dream at all but a premonition. The kiss, everything, was pure magic.

She heard footsteps outside her door and sat up. *Who could be walking around at this hour?* she wondered.

Suddenly the door crashed open. Elizabeth lifted her head in alarm. Out of the corner of her eye she saw Celine get up out of her bed.

"Celine!" Elizabeth cried.

Her body went rigid with fear as four strong hands closed around her wrists and ankles. She began struggling but was pinned to the bed.

"Celine!" she cried again.

She heard a familiar voice: "Celine, get out of here. The car is waiting downstairs."

A powerful starburst of light exploded before her face, scorching her eyes like a miniature sun. She was totally blinded.

Elizabeth opened her mouth to scream, but before she could, everything went black.

Chapter Seven

Tom sat at his sprawling, paper-strewn desk at WSVU, thumping the end of his pencil against his forehead.

Where is she? he wondered, glancing at his watch for the hundredth time. It was early in the afternoon. Elizabeth was supposed to have met him here half an hour ago. They were going to do the final edit on the secret society piece, which was to be the feature story on this evening's news.

For the first time since he started working at WSVU, Tom felt butterflies in his stomach. He'd been nervous before, nervous about going in front of the camera. The usual stage fright stuff. And it wasn't as if this would be his first important story. After all, there was the one he and Elizabeth had done on the illegal recruiting in the SVU athletics department and the one that busted Sigma House for illegal hazing. Both stories had rocked the university. So he was no stranger to controversy.

No, his nervousness came from the sinking feeling that this time the story wasn't going to just disappear. He knew there was going to be a price to pay. And he didn't mind paying up. The problem was he didn't know how much it was going to cost.

He knew he'd lose friends, but they were people whom he'd already written off anyway: former fraternity brothers, FOG members. No, he knew better than to think it was just a matter of losing friends. That bunch didn't fool around. More important, William White didn't fool around. William White was a dangerous man.

And now I'm his adversary, Tom thought. *In more ways than one.* He was not only blowing the cover off the society but he'd fallen in love with the one girl William wanted.

So he knew where these butterflies came from. Not from nervousness. From dread.

Where is *she?* Tom huffed. It was unlike Elizabeth to be late for anything.

He decided he couldn't wait any longer. The film had to go to final print in an hour. As he went into the editing room a thought occurred to him.

She's holed up in the library doing some last-minute research. Typical Elizabeth. Covering all her bases. Making sure nothing was left out.

But underneath that neat explanation was another feeling that he couldn't identify. Or, rather, *wouldn't* identify. He didn't like to acknowledge fear.

Elizabeth, where on earth are you?

Elizabeth tried to steady her ragged breathing. She twisted her head left and right. She couldn't see a thing. It was like looking up into the night sky but without a moon or the stars. Total blackness. And all she could smell was the musty dankness of the burlap sack they'd stuck over her head. It smelled like a barn. She clenched her teeth to keep them from chattering with terror.

Her head ached from whatever they'd used to knock her out—some sort of gas or something.

"Who are you? Why are you doing this to me?" she asked the blackness.

Elizabeth had seen enough mysteries and detective stories to know that she needed to concentrate all her powers on listening, to locate where she was. She could be anywhere. She jostled a bit. There was the sound of tires on pavement and faraway traffic. *I'm in a car.* That much was clear.

145

She tried to bring her hand up to her head to feel where it hurt but found her hands were shackled together.

"Ohhhh," she groaned.

She heard a muffled giggle, a female giggle.

Who's that?

Elizabeth heard laughter. Three or four males. And that female. She had a sneaking suspicion who the female was. *Who else could it be?* she thought. *She was sleeping less than ten feet from me when these creeps burst in. I saw her get out of bed. As if she was waiting for them . . .*

"Celine," Elizabeth murmured to herself.

They must have heard her. The car filled with uncomfortable silence.

"Keep quiet, Ms. Wakefield," a muffled voice commanded. "We're preventing you from making the biggest mistake of your life."

Mistake? Elizabeth thought. Tom had told her about the secret society. To them, exposure would be the same thing as a death sentence. The "biggest mistake of her life" had to be the news piece on them. It had to be.

Keep calm, Elizabeth pleaded with herself.

"What mistake?" she asked innocently.

"What mistake?" someone mocked. That female again. Of course it was her.

"Celine? Is that you?"

Elizabeth heard a struggle, a voice being

muffled, as though someone was being gagged with a hand or piece of cloth. Then she heard someone break free.

"Get off, you moron!"

"Ouch, Celine, are you trying to kill me?"

"Quiet!" roared a voice. "Terrific, Celine. Now she knows who you are."

"Who cares? It's not going to matter anyway. You said she won't remember a *thing*."

"Celine?" Elizabeth pleaded. "Why are you doing this?"

"It's not me, honeybunch," Celine drawled. "You made yourself a bigger enemy than little ole me. You thought you were riding a horse, but you were really riding an elephant. You might say that you and me are just along for the ride. Except that I'm getting off. And you're just going to keep on riding, right into the sunset."

"Enough!" cried that same voice.

William, Elizabeth thought. *It has to be William.*

She thought of his eyes all over her, of herself tied up and blinded . . . powerless to defend herself. . . .

It started at the base of her spine—a tingling sensation of fear that worked its way up her back and into her arms until she shook with terror.

But she wouldn't cry. She wouldn't give them the pleasure.

147

"Where are you taking me?" she asked, trying to keep her voice steady.

The air around her suddenly sucked dry of oxygen. She could hardly breathe. The small car seemed to inflate with horrible laughter. Her head cracked against the door, then she felt herself flung back on the seat. Her shoulder burned where she'd hit. She thought maybe she'd dislocated it. She felt faint. She was losing consciousness.

Am I dying?

Fingers closed around her arms, probed her face, grasped her ankles.

Am I dying?

Tires squealing . . . more laughter . . . horn blaring . . . the car made a sharp turn . . . then another one . . . then another . . . then another.

Todd stared at the phone, shell-shocked, expecting it to ring again. He'd just received his second of two calls. The first was from the dean. He'd told Todd that he wouldn't be able to play ball this season, but he would be able to practice with the team. And he could remain at SVU. But he'd have to move out of the athletes' dorm into regular freshman housing. Todd's heart leapt. Just one season of sitting out? He needed a vacation anyway. He'd come back next year rested and strong. He felt like thanking the dean—it wasn't great news, but it wasn't awful.

Then, as soon as he put down the phone, it rang again. This time it was Mark. He was in his room. The dean had called him first. His news wasn't as good. Todd had received illegal scholarship money and preferential treatment, but Mark had received cold cash—and his brand-new Explorer. With evidence like that, there was little the university trustees could do. Mark had lost his eligibility for good. And they would seek a court order that would keep him from playing basketball for any other school. Without saying what he was going to do, Mark signed off quickly, saying only, "Good luck, buddy. And watch your back," then hung up.

Todd had always seen the world in terms of black and white, good and bad. But this news was mixed—he could play next year, but Mark couldn't, maybe not ever again—and he felt mixed up.

He needed to talk to someone.

He headed out of the dorm and through the main quad. He passed by Lauren's dorm without even looking up and entered the neighboring building, Dickenson Hall. He knew everything he did was on impulse. He thought the best way to deal with this was not to think at all but just react. *Listen to the heart,* he told himself. And his heart led him to Elizabeth's door.

That's strange, Todd thought.

The door was off its hinges, as if someone had kicked it in. He knocked on it for what seemed like an hour. When no one answered, he tried the knob, but it came off in his hands. Suddenly a little worried, he lifted the door and moved it aside.

The room was the same: Elizabeth's side as neat as ever, Celine's as catastrophic, a minefield of cigarette butts and mounds of dirty clothes. Chalking up the broken door to the broken heart of one of the Celine's Neanderthal dates, he didn't think anything more of it. He scribbled out a note and left it on Elizabeth's pillow.

Good news—sort of.
Todd

Alex had completed every children's game on the coffee shop's paper place mat: the color by numbers, the ticktacktoe, and the connect-the-dots. Now she was shredding them up, tearing off little slivers of paper and rolling them into balls. The table looked like a battlefield after a spitball war.

Two hours ago she had received a collect call from Mark. He wouldn't say where he'd been. All he said was to meet him here. Now it was almost noon, and he was an hour late.

And Alex was already on her third cup of coffee. She'd been watching upperclassmen drinking it all semester to keep them awake in the library and give them a jolt before exams. She had started drinking it herself, and it drove her nuts—gave her the shakes and made her mind race a mile a minute. The caffeine lifted her mood to treetop level, then dropped it without warning, until she felt like crawling under a rock. But if she had just enough, she could stay really happy—even elated—for a whole morning. The only thing was, she hadn't had anything to eat since the day before yesterday, the last time she saw Mark. On an empty stomach coffee's effects had double or triple the impact. Some people could drink coffee just before they went to bed. But for Alex, it was like a drug.

She lifted her cup and took another sip. This jolt went straight to her brain. Her hand began to shake. Some of the coffee spilled. She put down the cup and turned toward the window, praying that she wouldn't lose this high before Mark got there.

In the distance the bell above the SVU chapel signaled twelve o'clock. Alex was bursting with anxiety as she watched the flow of happy students pass the window, heading for the academic buildings. They were laughing, poking each other in the ribs, goading each other about last night or last weekend. They looked like they didn't have a care in the world. Alex couldn't believe that only a few weeks ago she had been one of them.

If only Elizabeth hadn't done that story, she thought. *My life would be perfect.*

Somehow those words weren't as comforting as they usually were. They rang shrill and false in her mind. Maybe it was the coffee. But suddenly everything was crystal clear. Truths started falling down on her like rain.

Who am I kidding? My bubble had to burst sometime: after all, I'm Enid Rollins. Did I really think that changing my name to Alex would change everything?

Out of the corner of her eye Alex saw Mark's black Explorer pull up. Her heart sank. The car was so weighed down, the rear tires looked almost flat. All of Mark's belongings—clothes and basketballs and shoes and everything else that was familiar to her—were smashed against the back windows.

Alex felt a single tear trace its way down her cheek.

It's over, she said to herself.

She straightened up and wiped her face. She didn't want Mark to see her like this. She wanted him to think she could get along without him . . . even if she couldn't.

"Hi, Alex," Mark said awkwardly. He stood

over the table, his hands deep in his pockets. He looked nervous.

He's not even going to sit down to say it, Alex thought.

"Don't you want to sit down?" she asked. She wished she hadn't opened her mouth. She sounded pathetic. She gulped more coffee for another injection of artificial happiness.

Mark hesitated, then sat. His expression was as cold and sharp as the blade of a knife.

"So," Alex said.

"So."

"How was your trip?"

"Okay."

"Where'd you go? Big Sur?"

Mark sat stone still.

"Tijuana?"

Mark shrugged and stared blankly over Alex's shoulder.

"Mark, this is ridiculous. Aren't you even going to tell me where you've been?"

"I'm not married to you, you know," Mark snapped.

Alex looked around, embarrassed. People at the surrounding tables were glancing their way. She felt her caffeine high spin away down an invisible drain.

"Do you have to humiliate me in public, too?" she whispered across the table.

"I lost my eligibility, and my scholarship," Mark responded.

"Don't change the subject."

"That *is* the subject," Mark insisted. "That's the only subject."

"Anyway, that's not what Todd said yesterday," Alex said.

"I spoke to Todd this morning. The committee made the decision last night."

Alex paused and held her breath. "And Todd?"

Mark shook his head slowly, as if Todd were a hometown hero just killed in a faraway war. He shifted in his seat and wouldn't look Alex in the eyes. He just spoke into his hands. "I think I have a shot at making the NBA," he said quietly. "But I have to play some semipro ball first. I have a tryout in L.A. Tomorrow."

"Tomorrow?" She could barely get the word out.

"There's nothing left for me here."

This was it. This was what Alex had been waiting for. But no matter how much she'd prepared herself for it, it hit harder than she expected.

"What about me, Mark? What about us?"

Mark gave her a sad, crooked smile, leaned forward and kissed her once on the lips, then got up and walked away.

154

Alex didn't breathe until she heard the engine in Mark's Explorer turn over, then roar away and fade down the street.

As the policeman guarding Mike's hospital room opened the door and stepped aside, Jessica stood on the threshold. She couldn't bring herself to walk into the room. She was terrified by what she saw. Inside, Mike was sprawled unconscious in the bed. His face was attached to half a dozen different tubes and wires. They looked like biting things. He looked like some sort of insect, like the man in that story she read in high school by Kafka, who wakes up in the morning to find that he had turned into an insect.

Jessica's heart sank and she felt tears flooding her eyes again. *I swear, I've done enough crying in the last two days for a full lifetime,* she thought bitterly.

Standing there, she felt tugged in opposite directions by competing loyalties. On the one hand, she didn't want to go to the man who had tried to kill her brother. On the other, the man who had tried to kill her brother was Mike McAllery, the man she'd fallen in love with. And married.

Suddenly she felt the urge to protect him. It was like a *need* she had, an instinctive reaction.

155

Something she had no control over.

Jessica strode in and sat beside the bed.

The sound of the respirator was hypnotizing. She found herself staring into Mike's face—what she could see of it.

He looks so peaceful when he's asleep, she thought. *Like a little boy.*

So often during the night, she'd woken beside Mike in their bed and propped herself on her elbow and watched him breathe deeply. In the soft streetlight flowing through the window, she'd lost herself gazing at his dark, fluttering eyelashes. Then it seemed they had nothing but bright, happy futures before them. Life was perfect. She dreamed about him when she slept . . . she dreamed about him when she was awake.

But the dream was over.

Mike lay unconscious before her, being fed through tubes, breathing through a mask. Fighting for his life.

While she watched him, she played their relationship through her mind. From the time he leapt from the shadows and saved her from being attacked at the Homecoming dance, to the time she'd tailed him to Mojo's Bar and Grill and caught him in an embrace with a mysterious redhead, to the wonderful dinner they'd hosted together for Elizabeth and Tom, to every single time he'd gotten drunk and violent, to the final night. The night of that last terrible fight when she'd fled to Steven's apartment . . . her strangled cry . . . the gunshot.

Jessica shuddered as she heard it again. When she focused her eyes on Mike he was staring at her. She almost screamed in alarm.

"Mike, you're awake!"

Mike's eyelids fluttered a little, as though they were heavier than lead. His eyes kept moving around the room, then landed on Jessica again. A small smile appeared on Mike's cracked lips. His hand rose off the bed, but then fell back down. Too heavy.

"Don't try to move, Mike," Jessica said. She hesitated, then brought herself to put her hand on his. "Is this what you wanted?"

Mike managed a nod. Jessica felt a single, swollen finger wrap around one of hers. He stared up at the ceiling. His eyes filled with tears. One or two trickled down the side of his face.

Jessica braced herself. What she wanted more than anything at that moment was to throw her arms around his neck and turn back the clock. Turn it back to last week, before the last terrible fight. No, before that, before he'd started drinking so much. No, before that, to the moment she'd said yes when he asked her to marry him. To the moment he'd asked her to move in with him. Take it all back. Return to what seemed to matter most, that first jolt of love.

Jessica's eyes filled with hot tears. She wanted to find the one place where it had gone all wrong and fix it. She wanted Mike. She did. But not like this. And not like he was.

What do I really want?

"I—I—" Mike croaked. "Wa-water."

Jessica fed him a couple of sips of water from a paper cup to moisten his lips. His eyes fluttered again.

"Jess," he whispered. "Baby. I—I love you."

Jessica froze. Her heart was pounding, saying one thing, while her head was shouting for attention, saying another.

"I'm sorry. More than sorry," Mike said in a hoarse whisper. "I never meant to hurt you."

"Don't talk so much, Mike," Jessica said gently. "You need your strength."

"Don't care about strength," he whispered. "Look—" Mike's eyes closed for a moment, his breathing paused. Jessica looked on with horror. She thought Mike was dying then and there. But all of a sudden he came to again.

"B-baby," Mike went on. "It's all different now."

"Shh."

"You don't understand. I deserved what I got. I don't blame your brother. I don't need to forgive him because it's my fault, not his."

"He doesn't blame you," Jessica said. "Quiet. Save your strength."

"Things have changed," Mike continued. He looked down the length of his body to his legs. They lay lifeless under the blanket.

Jessica rested a hand on his knee.

"I don't feel that," Mike murmured to himself. He gripped Jessica's hand as hard as he could. "I understand if you want to leave me. I can't feel your hand on my knee, Jess. I—I might not walk again."

Mike turned his head and stared deep into Jessica's eyes. "I'll do anything if you'll stay with me, baby," he said. "You're my wife. I'll do whatever it takes. I'll testify in court that all this was an accident. Your brother will be free. I'll never drink again. It'll be different."

But all Jessica could do was stare at his lifeless legs. She hadn't really believed Mike's mother when she had said that Mike might not be able to walk. She'd thought it was just a scare tactic to get her down to the hospital.

But it's true. It's really true.

Elizabeth came to. She *had* fainted.

She fought off nausea as the car took one sharp turn after another.

"Look, maybe we should take her back now," a voice said. This one was also familiar.

"Peter?" Elizabeth called out into the car. "Peter Wilbourne, is that you?"

"Be quiet, Elizabeth," another voice said. "This is not a game. We are preventing you from making a mistake that would cost your life. We are saving your life."

"But what mistake?" Elizabeth demanded, struggling through another powerful wave of nausea. "I haven't done anything wrong."

"Not *yet*. But you and Watts are about to go too far," the voice said. "We require secrecy. We demand it."

"William," Elizabeth said slowly. "I know it's you. I never guessed you could be so cruel. The only mistake I've made is to let you near me. But I promise you, you are going to get exactly what you deserve."

"I agree," came William's cool reply. "I will get just what I deserve. And not a single thing less."

"The mistake is yours," Elizabeth whispered. "That story will air with or without me."

She could hear William laugh nervously. "That's absurd."

"It's taped. We filmed it last night. The story goes on at five o'clock."

The silence in the car was overpowering.

"You're bluffing," William said.

"Every time you've thought we were bluffing, you've been wrong," Elizabeth said in a ragged voice.

Silence.

Elizabeth knew she'd thrown them, and despite the fear in her stomach, she tried to feel confident.

"It's okay, darling," Elizabeth heard Celine say to William in a soothing voice. "It's a little story showing on some backwater college cable TV station. It's not a matter of life and death."

Silence.

Then she heard the throaty growl, like an animal's. "It is!" William roared. "A matter of life. And death!"

"William?" Celine pleaded. "Calm down."

"Get off me, Celine."

The car shrieked to a halt. Elizabeth was thrown forward to the floor.

". . . let's just kill her now . . ." she heard a voice say. An argument started swirling around her:

". . . let's get rid of her . . ."

". . . need her alive . . ."

". . . set her free . . ."

". . . last thing we need . . ."

". . . kill her! . . ."

The scream ripped through the car. "QUIET!"

No one said a word.

A chill climbed Elizabeth's spine again as she

161

remembered what Tom had told her. How much there was for the secret society to protect. How secrecy to them was everything. Without it they were nothing.

So it's come down to me or them, she realized. *One of us is going to die. And right now, I'm blindfolded, shackled, cold, and hungry. I don't know where I am . . . I don't have a chance.*

"Elizabeth," a voice, William White's, said coolly, calmly. "It's this simple. If you're telling the truth, if that story was taped, if it hits the air—you're dead."

Tom leaned back in his chair, drumming his fingers on the desk in WSVU's small studio. He chewed his lip and stared blankly at the camera.

Now he had a real problem. He looked up at the clock. It was only five minutes until news time. Fifteen minutes ago he was disappointed, because he'd really wanted to watch the show with Elizabeth. Ten minutes ago he was annoyed that Elizabeth would let him down like this. Now he was nervous.

If anything has happened to her, I don't know what I'll do, he told himself. *I shouldn't have let her out of my sight until this thing was over.* He raked his fingers through his hair one more time.

162

Oh well, he thought. *Here goes nothing.*

The red light on the camera went on. He made the usual introductory remarks.

"After these messages, an exclusive urgent report from field reporter Elizabeth Wakefield . . ."

Chapter Eight

Steven felt like a Roman emperor. Still tingling from a disinfectant bath, he was stretched out on the couch, his feet and head propped up on stacks of pillows. Billie ran back and forth to the kitchen, delivering his favorite foods one after another: chips and salsa, then chicken enchiladas, then a sausage-and-triple-cheese pizza. Steven's eyes were glued to an *L.A. Law* rerun.

"You have no idea how good it is to see color," he said to Billie between salsa runs. "In jail everything is gray. The walls, the bars, the floors, the prisoner uniforms, even the guard uniforms. When I got out today and saw the blue sky and the leaves, I almost started crying."

Home never felt so good after a night in the county jail, he thought. He caught Billie's eye.

"Maybe I should spend the night in jail more often."

Billie looked at him as if he had just sprouted a pair of antlers. "I think you got your brain rattled in there by some drunken lunatic," she said.

"It just makes you appreciate . . . well, everything," Steven said, gazing adoringly at Billie.

Billie shook her head. "I'd appreciate it if you found some other way to appreciate me than going to jail," she teased.

The phone rang.

"Let me get that, Your Highness," Billie said. She picked up the phone. "Jess!" she cried.

Steven lurched to his feet.

"I'll put him on," Billie said, then handed the phone to Steven. "I think it's good news," she whispered.

"Jess?"

"I'm at the hospital, with Mike," Jessica said.

Steven said nothing.

"He's going to pull through."

Steven's knees weakened with relief. He fell back onto the couch. Billie ran over to him, her face stricken with worry, but he gave her a thumbs-up.

"I guess that means I'm not a murderer," Steven said.

Jessica didn't answer right away. "You never would have been," she finally said. "You didn't do anything wrong."

"If only Mike thought so," said Steven. "I'd be free and clear."

"He does," Jessica said.

"He does what?"

"He thinks you didn't do anything wrong either. That's the other thing I wanted to tell you. Mike's agreed to testify on your behalf."

This time Steven almost passed out with relief. He closed his eyes as all the fears he'd built up during the long night in jail evaporated. He felt as light as air.

"I don't know what to say," he said, choking up.

"Say thank you," Jessica said.

She sounded strange, weirdly calm, too calm. As if there was something she wasn't saying. Steven's stomach tightened.

"What else, Jess?"

"What do you mean, what else?"

"I'm your brother," Steven reminded her. "I may not be as good as Elizabeth at guessing what you're thinking, but I can tell something's up."

"Mike may never walk again," Jessica said bluntly. "And I'm thinking of . . . I'm thinking of staying with him."

Steven held his tongue. If he had learned anything in the last few weeks, it was that bad things happened when you messed with someone else's life.

"I'm his wife," Jessica said. "It's my . . . *duty,* I guess. I don't know."

"You don't sound so sure," Steven said.

"I *am* sure!"

"Okay, Jess," Steven said, controlling himself.

"Okay?" Jessica said, confused.

"It's your life."

"It is?"

"You have to make your own decision," Steven insisted. He liked this new approach. It sounded smarter. And it was probably more productive.

"I do," Jessica agreed tentatively.

The phone filled with silence.

"Jess? Are you still there?"

"I'm here," came the meager reply. Jessica suddenly sounded far away. Steven knew that distant voice anywhere. That was his sister's confused voice, her confused and scared voice. She wasn't sure at all.

"Whatever you decide to do, Jess, I support it," Steven said.

"You do?"

"We're on the same team, remember?"

Silence. Then he heard a sound he'd recognize anywhere. Jessica was crying.

"We're here for you, Jess," Steven said lovingly. "Billie and I. Whenever you need us."

"Thanks," Jessica whispered.

"I love you, Jess."

"Bye, Steven."

"Bye."

Billie ran over, practically exploding with curiosity. "Well?"

Steven sat back on the couch and gazed thoughtfully into space. "Mike's going to live, but he may never walk again. And Jessica is thinking of staying with him."

Billie stood back, aghast. "And this is how you're reacting? Why aren't you ranting and raving?"

"Because it's her life," Steven said, pulling Billie into his lap and kissing her neck. "I have my own life. And it's just getting to the good part."

Billie playfully tweaked Steven's nose. "Hands off, you *con*-vict!" she commanded. "I only kiss *law*-abiding citizens."

"You always liked the bad guys better," Steven said. "Maybe I should have taken a lesson in looking tough from Mike."

Billie inspected him closely. "Maybe you're right. Maybe jail was good for you after all. What did they feed you? I'll put it on my shopping list."

Suddenly Steven found his eyes riveted to the TV screen. He leaned forward on the couch. "Hey!" he said, pointing. "It's Elizabeth!"

Billie laughed and shook her head. "Those Wakefield twins. Always making headlines. Always in the limelight."

For the fourth or fifth time that day Winston found himself blushing from head to toe. This time the embarrassment was total. He and Denise had plopped down next to Nina and Bryan in the common room of Oakley Hall to watch TV. A pile of women's magazines was sitting next to the couches. Denise picked one up and casually waved it in front of Winston's face.

"Remember this one, Winnie? Remember that fascinating article in here you told me about—'How Can He Tell What You're Thinking'? Or what about 'Ten Ways to Know If It's True Love'? Remember how you told me you gave yourself the test? I forget, did we pass or not?"

Winston melted into the pillows. Bryan and Nina let loose several minutes of laughter at Winston's expense.

"Egbert," Bryan said. "You *are* the smoothest operator I know."

"No, he's not," Denise said, circling her slender arms around Winston's neck. "But he tries."

Winston had to stop himself from sliding all the way to the floor. He'd been prepared to take his brand-new relationship with Denise public. He'd even been prepared to take a little kidding here and there. But he hadn't been prepared for Denise's talent at making him feel loved and foolish all at once. She acted like they'd been together not hours but years. It was like she knew him better than he knew himself, and he wasn't sure whether he liked that or not.

Denise was nuzzling him. He felt the cool circle her lips left on his neck as she pulled away. This he liked.

But he couldn't look at Bryan. Every time he did, Bryan gave him a big, meaningful wink. One of those guy things. Like: "Heh, heh, heh, I know what *you* two have been up to."

The funny thing was, Winston hadn't even tried to get very far with Denise the other night. They had fallen asleep in each other's arms before a stitch of clothing dropped to the floor. And that was just fine by him, although he had stocked his top drawer with condoms just in case. But every guy he'd seen since Denise gave him the Big Kiss at the charity ball had been sticking their bony elbows in his side. "So, Win . . ." Wink, wink, nudge, nudge.

He'd read something about that in one of those women's magazines. He'd been reading them religiously, hoping that one of them would give him useful advice on figuring out what was going on inside Denise's head. One article talked about how in the old days guys would court girls for months or even years before anything serious happened. But times had changed. Today it was boom-boom-boom: you meet, you kiss, you hop in the sack.

Not him and Denise, though. No way, over his dead body. He'd gotten his treasure, and he wanted to treat it right, move everything along gradually, the way it used to be. They wouldn't be rushed along by any "societal pressure" (that was what the psychologist quoted by the magazine called it). But the funny thing about the magazine was the way its cover girl was dressed: she didn't leave much to the imagination. Whose side were they on, anyway?

"Winnie, don't look so serious," Denise chided him.

Whose side are you *on?* Winston addressed the Denise in his mind. *Are you with them, or are you with me?*

Todd suddenly appeared in the doorway.

"Yo, Todd," Winston called. "Where've you been? I've been looking for you all day."

He put his arm around Denise's shoulders and smiled proudly.

"Okay, Romeo." Todd laughed. "I see her."

"Here we go, boys and girls," Nina said, leaning forward and turning up the volume of

172

the TV. "Everyone pay attention. Todd, you're just in time."

Elizabeth's face flashed across the screen.

"What's this all about?" Todd asked, sitting on the floor.

"Elizabeth didn't say," Nina replied. "But I have a sneaking suspicion. And if I'm right, this should be really good."

"*Really* good," Bryan echoed.

Celine jumped at William's enraged shout. There was Elizabeth on the television, giving the background on the story: the mysterious racial attacks on campus, the strange threats students had received, a history of unanswered rumors. But there was also Elizabeth sitting next to them. Two Elizabeths, one blindfolded, gagged, and bound at the wrists and the other free, singing like a songbird, and . . . *taped*.

William leapt to his feet, ripped off his mask, and snarled at the television. The veins in his neck pulsed, his hands closed into fists. All over Sweet Valley the secret society was being split open like a pomegranate: ". . . Fraternal Order of the Gallows . . . national organization . . . power extended all the way to Washington . . . locally represented by the Sigma fraternity . . . local leader: William White . . ."

William whirled and paced the room, growling like a savage animal, waving his hands wildly in the air. He stopped in front of the blinded Elizabeth, his eyes flashing. He reached out and closed his hands around an invisible throat, choking it, strangling . . .

After Elizabeth signed off, Todd still sat at Winston's feet, apparently totally entranced by the blank television screen. But he still saw her image, like a ghost: her long golden blond hair, her serious sea-green eyes. *She's so beautiful,* he said to himself. *Was she always so beautiful?*

He was incredibly proud of her. The charges she'd made were serious. And it looked as if she had her facts right. But then she had just vanished from the screen like she'd vanished from his life. One minute she was there, she was everything; the next minute gone. Poof.

"Todd? Hello?" It was Winston, shaking him by the shoulder.

Todd realized everyone was looking at him, wondering how he would react to seeing his old flame so obviously thriving without him.

"Some story. Well, gotta go," he said quickly. "See you guys around."

Winston followed him out. "Speaking of stories," he said, "how'd your meeting go with the dean?"

"Don't look so sad, Win," Todd said, realizing almost immediately that he was talking to himself. "It's not like it's my funeral or anything."

"Yeah, I know," Winston said. "We're just worried about you, that's all."

"Thanks," Todd replied. "Well, it could have been worse. I can't play ball this season, but I can next season. And I have to move out of the dorm."

"That's it?"

"That's it."

Winston shook Todd's hand. "May I congratulate you, sir?"

"Maybe I should congratulate *you*," Todd said, nodding in Denise's direction. Then he winked.

Winston frowned. "Why does everybody do that?"

"Do what?"

"Wink! It's like when anyone sees us together, they get dirt in their eye or something."

"I don't know, Win." Todd sighed heavily. "Old habits die hard, I guess."

Winston looked at him as if he knew he wasn't just talking about winking. "There's something else on your mind?"

"I don't want to bother you with it," Todd said. "You have other things to think about."

"Try me."

"You won't believe it."

"Maybe not, but then again I never believed I'd ever get Denise, either."

"Okay," Todd said. He took a deep breath. "I want Elizabeth back."

It felt great just to say it out loud. It was as if telling someone made him even more certain it was true. He said it again. "I want Elizabeth back."

"That's not hard to believe," Winston said. "With a woman like Elizabeth, you'd be an idiot not to."

"I can't stand it, Win. I just can't stand it anymore. But I have to go. I'll see you around." He turned to go.

"What are you going to do, Todd?" Winston called out.

Todd whirled around. He didn't even have to think. "Whatever it takes."

Elizabeth struggled to free herself. William's lunatic howl rebounded off the cavelike walls, echoing throughout the chamber.

"Stop!" Celine cried out, clamping her hands over her ears.

For the first time since she'd been involved with William and the secret society, she felt afraid. She'd seen the real William now. All that coolness was a front. She knew he'd just as soon kill Elizabeth as he would a fly: without guilt, without thinking of the consequences. It was one thing to *want* to kill somebody. How many times had she herself wished Elizabeth would just dry up and blow away? But it was another thing to actually do it.

Celine watched Elizabeth struggle in her chair, twisting her wrists against the knots, trying to kick her feet free.

She's so brave, Celine said to herself, then stopped, realizing that was the first nice thought she had ever had about her roommate. Elizabeth had always been Little Miss Perfect, self-righteous and stuck up. And all that straight, angelic blond hair. She was sickening, like oversweet candy. But it took driving right up to the edge to show Celine her mistake. Elizabeth was a pain in the neck, but she didn't deserve to die for it.

William marched straight for Celine and backed her against the wall. He grabbed her by the arms and glared deep into her eyes.

"Are you with us, Celine?" William seethed. "Are you still with us? Because if you're not, I have another chair, another six feet of rope. You either help us get rid of her or you join her!"

Celine opened her mouth to scream, but nothing came out. William had lost it, his control, his intelligence—his mind. All that sophistication was a front. Beneath all that ice he was a throbbing animal. A menace. To Elizabeth. To *her*.

William tightened his grip on Celine's arms. She could feel her feet leave the ground.

"William, you're hurting me!"

"What's it going to be?"

"My arms!"

"What! The answer! Now!"

"Yes!" Celine screamed.

"Yes what?"

"I'm with you!"

William released her. But as Celine fell to the floor she knew she wasn't. She wasn't with William. She wasn't with anybody.

Elizabeth felt a hand grab at the sack over her head and rip it off. She saw bright lights, stars, shadows, like she'd been punched. Her clothes were drenched with sweat from her struggle with the ropes. Muffled voices came from all directions. She had no idea how much time had passed. She didn't remember anything after the car stopped. Had they knocked her out again? She knew who her captors were, but not where they'd taken her.

Her vision started coming back. She saw a dimly lit room with a low ceiling. Stone walls. A dirt floor. She was in a chair with her arms

178

bound behind her. Several people surrounded her, wearing black hoods with slits for eyes and a mouth. They looked like hangmen for the gallows. But from the neck down they were their regular selves. She would know three of those bodies anywhere: William White, Peter Wilbourne, and Celine. Two others she thought she recognized as Sigma thugs.

"Let's stop playing games, William," Elizabeth said slowly. "I've seen you now. I know who you all are. The rest of you can take off the Halloween costumes."

"It doesn't matter if you know," William said, his ice blue eyes raging with anger. "You won't be alive to tell the tale."

The others ripped off their masks. William's narrow lips were quivering. Peter looked his same dull self. But Celine had changed. She looked undone, with her mascara running, her hair tousled, her lipstick smudged. She wouldn't look Elizabeth in the eye.

"I should have stopped you before," William hissed. "I should have arranged a nice little accident. Now I'm going to have to kill you myself. You really disappointed me, Elizabeth. I thought you were a woman of class and honor. But now I see that you're just a cheap, two-bit freshman *fool*. Just like your sister, who fell for that gutter trash McAllery."

To insult her was one thing, but to lash out at her sister was unbearable. Elizabeth struggled to free her hands but failed. She aimed her toe at the base of William's knee and fired a kick. The point of her boot struck bone, and William growled and clutched his knee. Elizabeth wanted to shout at him, but her throat was blocked with a poisonous bile of fear and anger.

William stood, his whole body now quaking with tension, the whites of his eyes demon red. Then, suddenly, his face deadened into an uneasy calm. A razor-thin, diabolical smile cracked the suface.

He turned to Peter. "It's a shame. Another SVU freshman commits suicide. We'll have to organize an awareness seminar to combat this terrible epidemic."

Peter's laugh was uncertain.

Elizabeth looked from face to face. Her eyes passed over Celine's, then went back. There was something in Celine's expression. Something new. A sign?

Could Celine actually want to help her?

Celine looked wildly around the room, hoping to discover an ally. But they all stared up at William in obedience, ready to leap off the Empire State Building if their leader told them to. She looked at Peter, his eyes glued to

William, at William's beck and call as always. She could still feel his beard scrubbing her face like sandpaper.

What a spineless wimp, she said to herself. As she looked at them she realized she had made out with just about every male in the room. She glared at them all, remembering what she hated about each one. That one's fingers were studded with calluses; that one's shoulders were powdered in drifts of dandruff.

They're all spineless wimps, she declared silently.

And then William. He was pointing his long, bony finger at Elizabeth, working himself into a frenzy.

"You, my dear," he was saying, shaking with rage, "are going to suffer a long, slow end."

He's . . . he's . . . he's an absolute maniac.

Celine looked around the cave. She had to think. She had to buy some time.

"I've, uh . . . I've got to go outside for a cigarette," she mumbled, heading quietly for the secret exit.

Just as the red light on the camera went dark and the cameraman gave Tom a thumbs-up, the telephone rang across the TV studio. Tom leapt from behind the anchor desk and grabbed it on the second ring.

It had to be Elizabeth. Either that or someone calling to complain about the show. The complainers always called the second Tom signed off, like they were watching the television with their hand on the phone. They always had some stupid little peeve. They didn't like his shirt, or the way his hair was combed. And once in a while someone called with a tip, more information on certain parts of a story he might have left out. This time, though, he was sure it was Elizabeth. She had probably had just enough time to catch the show at home after staying in the library all day.

"Elizabeth?" He'd barely got the phone to his mouth before he'd blurted her name.

There was no answer.

"Elizabeth?" Tom heard only heavy breathing. He hated these pranks worse than the old ladies who were offended by the design of his tie.

"Hello?"

Tom thought he heard someone crying. A shudder surged through him. "Who is this?" he demanded.

"It's Celine."

"Celine!" *Not you,* he said to himself. *I can't deal with this right now.* "Look, I can't stay on the phone. I'm expecting an important call—"

Tom didn't finish his sentence. He heard Celine sobbing in the background.

"Come on, Celine! This isn't the time for your stupid games. Elizabeth—"

"She won't be calling," Celine said, her voice wavering.

For the first time since he had known Celine, Tom thought he detected something different in her voice. None of that Southern sass now. If he hadn't known better, he would have said Celine sounded afraid.

"Celine, you better not be—"

"I don't have much time," Celine whispered quickly. Her voice was breathy and strained. She *was* afraid. "They don't know I'm calling you."

"They? Who's they?"

Silence. That could mean only one thing. Tom felt his heart plummet.

"They have her," Celine said. "They have Elizabeth here."

"Where? Where are you, Celine? Tell me."

"He said . . . he said he's going to kill her! Oh, Tom, I don't know what to do."

"Celine. Celine! Get a grip on yourself. *Who* said he's going to kill her?"

"William," Celine sniffled. "William White."

William White! Tom didn't think William was capable of killing someone, but maybe he'd underestimated him.

"Celine, calm down, okay? William can't know you called me. You have to go back in there and act like nothing happened. Do you understand?"

Celine whimpered on the other end of the line.

"If you ever had it in you to do anything good, Celine, this is the time. You've got to get ahold of yourself. Do you understand?"

There was silence.

"Do you understand?" Tom repeated.

"Just hurry," came the whispered reply.

"Now tell me where you are. I'm coming, and I'm bringing the police with me!"

Chapter Nine

Jessica hadn't moved from Mike's hospital bed. He'd been in and out of consciousness all day. Every time he opened his eyes, he gripped Jessica's hand with that same single finger. And he would catch his breath. His eyes would brim with tears. Jessica had never seen him so vulnerable or needy. Then he'd nod off again.

She'd been trying to sleep herself. But every time she got near, she was wakened by a jolt of reality. She knew the time had come to make the hardest decision of her life.

She was completely exhausted. She had no idea what time it was, but she was too worked up for sleep. Too tormented. This time there was no Elizabeth to bail her out, no way around it, no escape.

The problem was that every time she came

up with another reason to stay with him, she came up with one to leave him. The list for both choices was growing longer.

Too much has happened, she would think. *He's hurt me one too many times. He's a drunk and he's unpredictable and he's dangerous. And he tried to kill poor Steven, who was only trying to protect me. I wonder if I ever loved him?* she asked herself. *I know I was crazy about him. But is being head over heels the same as love?*

That seemed to her an important thing to figure out. She would stare at her shattered husband a long, long time. And as she stared she would feel that pang of responsibility again. And then the list of reasons to stay with him would grow another notch or two:

He's wild—that's exactly why I fell in love with him in the first place. Life with him would never be a fairy tale: the big house, the three kids, the dog, the two cars in the driveway. It wouldn't ever be that fairy tale, but it might be another one: life with Mike McAllery would never be predictable, but it would never be dull.

The fantasies flooded her mind: motorcycle rides along the beach in the moonlight, midnight dashes into the water . . .

Wait a second! she commanded herself. She opened her eyes. Mike lay completely still in the hospital bed. She gazed at the deadened limbs that were once his strong, quick legs.

*What am I talking about? No more motorcycle.
No more dashing around. Mike is paralyzed. Get
that into your thick skull. Mike will never walk
again!*

The thought was harsh, but it was realistic:
Do I want to live with that for the rest of my life?

The time of reckoning was definitely here.
She had to think hard. She had to think honestly. And when it came to Mike McAllery, honesty didn't come easily. But she'd try.

She closed her eyes and commanded herself
to be honest. Really, completely one hundred
percent truthful.

She opened her eyes as a new thought invaded her mind. As much as he'd frightened her
when he got drunk or lost his temper, she knew
that the trouble they were in wasn't completely
his fault. She couldn't lay the whole thing at his
feet.

Okay, good, Jessica. There's a good place to
start.

Yes, he was childish, he was violent, he was
overprotective and selfish, she knew. But she
had known all that when she married him.
Those things really hadn't been what drove
them apart. If she was being *really* honest with
herself, what drove them apart was the fact that
Mike wanted more than she could give. She just

187

wasn't ready for this sort of life. She was just a freshman in college beginning to explore the freedom of adulthood. Instead of feeling like Mike's princess, she'd felt like Rapunzel, trapped in a small room at the top of a tall tower while life went on for everyone else below.

All this honesty was giving her a headache.

Jessica put her hand on his thigh. It still felt muscular and powerful. She couldn't believe it wouldn't move by itself again.

Then she saw it. Or she thought she saw it. Out of the corner of her eye, she thought she saw Mike's leg move. A twitch. Not more than a reflex. But she was sure there was movement. She stared at it, trying to will it to move again. She was afraid to blink, thinking she'd miss it. But nothing happened.

Maybe I'm just seeing things, she thought. *When am I finally going to learn that things don't happen just because I want them to?*

Jessica sighed. "I'm your wife," she said to his unconscious figure as hot tears streaked down her face. "Till death do us part. Isn't that what we said? Didn't I promise you that, Mike?"

Todd's palms were sweating and his heart was pounding as he ran up the steps of Dickenson Hall. After leaving Winston and the others, he knew he had to try Elizabeth's room one more time. He had to see her tonight and tell her he still loved her.

But when he reached her room, he stood in amazement in front of the door. It hadn't been repaired. It was in the exact position he'd left it.

"That's strange," he said to himself. "Why hasn't she gotten that fixed?"

He lifted the door aside and went into the room. Nothing inside had changed either. His note was still on Elizabeth's desk. No one had been there all day.

"You'd think with the door wide open like that one of them would have stayed here to keep an eye on things," he muttered to himself. "That's *really* not like Elizabeth." He frowned.

Todd's heart began to pound a little harder, this time not out of love but out of a sense that something was wrong. He started adding up the clues, one after the other: the smashed-in door, the unread note, the strange silence from Elizabeth . . . the news story about the dangerous secret society.

"If they're so dangerous, why isn't she afraid?" he asked the empty room. "Why isn't she in danger?" His eyes narrowed. His handsome face hardened. "Or is she?"

He still thought it was his place . . . his right . . . Elizabeth was still his.

With the power and speed of an athlete,

Todd bolted out of the room and into the night.

Tom dug his fingers into the backseat of the police cruiser. He could see the blue and red emergency lights of the car he was in and the three or four cars that followed. The flashing lights sliced through the peaceful dark of the windows and doorways, as the cars sped to the other side of campus. Out of the police radio squawked the dispatcher's urgent commands, ordering other units to the location Tom had given them.

Tom went over and over in his mind what he could have done differently. Could he have done anything short of actually killing William before he killed anyone else?

Maybe it was just his fate to lose people. First his family. And now Elizabeth. And it was always his fault, always because of him. Elizabeth never would have gotten so close to the secret society if he hadn't given her any leads. He could have steered her away. Made a deal with William even.

What if he was too late? What if she . . .

Stop it! Tom commanded himself. *I've got to save her!* He held hands over his ears to stop the voices in his head. He trained his eyes straight ahead, between the two policemen riding up front. The cruiser's headlights spotlit their target.

"Stop here!" he cried to the policemen. "The Sigma house!"

Tom leapt out of the car and led the six police officers through a thick stand of trees.

"How do you know where you're going, son?" the sergeant asked.

"Later," Tom panted. "No time to explain."

Todd rammed his shoulder against the entrance to WSVU. The door shuddered but didn't give. He ran around to the back. The shades to all the windows were drawn. He rattled all the doorknobs, but the doors were all locked. He returned to the front and eyed the door like a bull ready to charge. He took four big steps away, lowered his shoulder, and took off like a sprinter exploding out of the blocks.

The next thing he knew he was lying faceup on the ground, seeing stars. He couldn't tell which stars were real and which were swimming around in his head. He didn't know how much time had passed. Maybe a second, maybe an hour. He got up woozily. Everything hurt. But the door was busted wide open, cracked across the middle.

He stepped inside. All the desks were deserted, all the blank computer screens stared at him through the dark. "Wrong decision, you idiot," they all seemed to be saying in chorus. "She's not here."

"Shut up!" Todd shouted, and rubbed his head. He felt a lump the size of an orange blossoming on his forehead. He thought his shoulder might be dislocated. But now wasn't the time to gripe about minor aches and pains. All those years he'd spent with Elizabeth, and now their entire future together was at stake.

He glared back at each computer screen. *They see everything. If they could only talk,* he said to himself. *Tell me!* he wanted to shout. *Where is she?*

Okay. Calm down. Think. If Elizabeth is in trouble, it's got to be with the secret society. And who are they? She said some of them belong to a fraternity, the Sigmas. Sigma House!

Todd spun and plunged back into moonlight. Over the far side of campus the sky was ablaze with red and blue lights, shifting and flashing like the northern lights. *Or a huge fire,* Todd thought . . . *Or police emergency lights.*

Celine sucked in her breath. Two of William's goons took Elizabeth by her arms and started dragging her toward the center of the floor.

"Pull the rope, Wilbourne," William commanded.

Peter Wilbourne yanked on a rope that operated an ancient winch. Like magic, a trapdoor slid aside. The floor opened up and revealed a pit of pitch darkness that had no visible bottom. The goons continued dragging Elizabeth toward it. She kicked at the dirt. Pebbles and clumps of old sod rained into the pit—the famous pit that Sigma pledges feared worse than any other fate.

Everyone heard it at the same time: a delayed splash. The pit was filled with water! And what else? Snakes? Rats?

Celine shuddered. She hated snakes more than anything in the world: their long, slimy, slithering bodies.

"Celine!" Elizabeth shrieked, reaching out toward Celine as she slid closer and closer . . .

Celine Boudreaux, Celine commanded herself, *if you ever do one good thing in your life, let this be it!* She raised her eyes toward the ceiling. *I'm sorry for everything down and dirty I've ever done. I take back every bad thing I've ever said about you. Please, God, don't let this happen to Elizabeth.*

Then she thought she heard an inner voice: "You can do it, Celine. You can save her."

"But how?" she wailed, looking about wildly. "How?"

*   *   *

Tom reached into the leaves and yanked up a steel trapdoor that led into an underground bunker and guided the police officers inside.

Underground, the corridor was too low to stand in. Water trickled from the ceiling and slithered down the walls, forming narrow streams and brooks that they had to leap over. Torch flames lined the craggy rocks, filling the small space with enlarged, grotesque shadows. Here and there carvings were etched into a doorway, dates from as far back as 1898.

Tom and the police officers raced along, stooping and skipping down the corridor, until they were blocked by an immense wooden door. Carved deep into it was a symbol that wasn't so strange to Tom: the broken star.

They could hear voices on the other side. Then silence. Then the piercing, terrified scream of a young woman.

Oh, Elizabeth, he thought desperately, his heart aching. *I'm coming for you. Please hold on.*

The police officers frantically searched the door with their flashlights. There was no doorknob. There were no hinges. This was no door. It was a barricade, built to keep away the outside world. Permanently.

Elizabeth slashed at her captors' hands. She dragged her nails savagely through skin and one hand and was dropped. Someone retreated into the shadows.

"You incompetent!" William cried. He turned to Peter Wilbourne. "Throw her in!" he commanded. "Afterward, we'll dump her outside. It will look like she just jumped into the gorge."

Peter took hold of Elizabeth's wrist and began to tug.

"Peter, stop!" Elizabeth cried. "You don't have to listen to him."

Peter paused. He looked confused. He seemed to be losing confidence.

"Wilbourne!" William thundered.

"You don't have to do what he says, Peter!" Elizabeth said. "Do you want to ruin everything you've ever worked for? Do you want to spend the rest of your life in jail?"

William shook with rage. "Do as I say, Wilbourne!"

They all heard it at the same time. The thumping on the door. The muffled shouts. Elizabeth could hear Tom crying out to her. He sounded so far away. Then there it was, as though from a far distance: "Open up. Police!"

"I'm in here!" Elizabeth cried. "Help!"

"Shut up!" William ordered her. "Wilbourne, you fool. I'll do it myself." He shoved Peter aside and began pushing Elizabeth toward the edge of the pit.

*　　*　　*

"We can't get through, Sarge," one of the officers complained. They were butting at the thick door with their shoulders, pounding on it with their fists. But what they really needed was a battering ram. From the other side they could all hear Elizabeth's tortured screams.

"Elizabeth!" Tom cried, hurling himself against the door. "Elizabeth, hold on!" But it was like throwing himself at the side of a cliff. The door was built to be opened only from the inside. And he knew that the secret society had an escape route. It seemed hopeless.

Suddenly, miraculously, they heard the door groan and watched it shudder. They stepped back. A crack of light shot out from the edge. Then it widened. Again Tom threw himself at the door with a strength powered by a rush of adrenaline. The door shuddered again and swung open.

And in the opening appeared a beautiful face twisted with fear, with tears cascading down swollen cheeks.

"Celine!" Tom cried. He looked at her as though seeing her for the first time. Or at least seeing something else in her for the first time. He nodded, then pushed her out of the way. He and the police officers poured into the dungeon like water rushing down a drain.

*   *   *

Celine slid behind the door and watched from the shadows. The secret society brothers scattered and ran in confused circles. The police officers swarmed in and grabbed at them. Peter Wilbourne threw his hands in the air the first chance he got and fell to his knees. He practically kissed the feet of the policeman who took him into custody.

Eventually the others gave themselves up. The policemen's guns were obviously convincing.

But where were William and Elizabeth? When the chaos died down they were nowhere to be seen.

Suddenly Tom broke away from the pack of blue uniforms and flashing badges and streaked across the cavelike room toward the shadows at the opposite end. A last of glimpse of Elizabeth was visible before she was dragged around the corner. *The escape route!* Celine thought urgently.

Two police officers leapt to their feet and drew their guns. But it was too late. William and Elizabeth were gone.

Tom took a running jump and hurdled the dark pit. He seemed to hover over the gaping hole for a frightening second before he cleared it, like he was frozen in time. His instincts had come back to him when he needed them most.

Who, Celine wondered as Tom vanished into the shadows, *would come to save me?*

An explosion of shouts and terrified screams.

"Tom!" Celine heard Elizabeth cry.

Then the three of them—Tom, Elizabeth, and William—tumbled out into the light.

Tom had William clamped in a headlock, and William had Tom around the waist. Elizabeth was caught between them, trying to struggle free.

Tom bent down to pull Elizabeth out of William's grip and push her to safety.

Elizabeth screamed as William's fist cracked against Tom's jaw. Tom reeled back and William punched him again.

"Tom!" Elizabeth shrieked, struggling to her feet.

Tom fell to the ground and William came after him. Elizabeth hurled herself at William.

It gave Tom the time he needed. He got to his feet and punched William with such force William staggered backward, perilously close to the mouth of the pit. With speed and agility Tom wrapped an arm around William's neck. His grip was so tight that William gasped for breath. William's face grew white. His body went limp.

Is Tom going to kill him? a voice in Celine's head was shouting.

Tom's eyes were strangely vacant, distant. Tom seemed to be beating not only William but all of his frustrations, all of his mysterious pain—it was as if destroying William White would erase his own past.

Choking sounds rose from William's throat.

Elizabeth grabbed Tom's arm. "Tom!" she cried. "Tom, you're killing him!"

Tom squeezed harder. William's eyes closed.

"Tom, stop!" Elizabeth shrieked.

It was Elizabeth's voice that broke the spell. Just when it looked like it was too late, Tom's eyes focused and he released William.

William collapsed on the floor, heaving for air.

Tom reached for Elizabeth and held her. He rocked her in his arms, oblivious to the policemen who had surrounded them with pistols drawn, oblivious to the shouts and whispers around them.

Oblivious even to William, who'd gotten to his feet and made a last terrifying lunge at Tom and Elizabeth.

Elizabeth cried out. Tom threw William so hard he stumbled backward.

Everyone heard William's echoing cry as he fell into the yawning pit. And then silence.

Celine waited for the sound of the body hitting the ground. It didn't come.

A single pale hand with long, bony fingers

rose out of the blackness, clawing at the loose dirt. Tom released Elizabeth, raced toward the edge, and grabbed hold of William's wrist.

Tom held it, staring at William's hand.

"Pull me up, you idiot!" William ordered.

Tom looked around at all the faces: the police officers', the society members', Celine's, Elizabeth's. Her eyes were glued to him, telling him wordlessly what to do.

He peered down at William, whose feet were dangling over the abyss.

"Help me, fool!" came William's strangled cry.

"Give me a reason," Tom said. "Give me a single reason I should save you."

"Because you don't have the guts to drop me," William hissed. "Because you're weak! You're all weak!"

Tom peered down. "Death is too good for you, White," he said through gritted teeth. "I want the pleasure of seeing you suffer."

Then Tom yanked, grabbed hold of one arm, then the other, and with all his strength pulled William up. But before he pulled him to safety, he held William by the arms out over the edge of the pit.

"I want you to know something, White," Tom said.

William's face went ash gray as he looked down and behind him.

"I want you to remember what this is like. How does it feel to be powerless? How does it feel to be in the hands of someone who would just as well see you dead as alive? I'm letting you live not because I'm weak, but because I want you to learn about powerlessness and pain. Remember that while you're sitting in your prison cell."

"I won't be going to prison, Watts," William sneered. "No one will be able to put me away."

Tom pulled William away from the pit and threw him to the ground.

The police officers rushed forward to handcuff him.

Dusty, his clothes torn, his face bloody, Tom stepped toward Elizabeth and wrapped her in his arms again, holding her as she sobbed. The look on Tom's face was so open, so full of love for Elizabeth that Celine looked away.

She took a sliding step toward the exit. Hoping no one would see her, she turned to run. The next thing she felt was her face smashing against what felt like a brick wall.

She recoiled against the blow and looked up and saw the blue jacket of the towering police sergeant.

"Not so fast," he said, turning her around against the wall and clamping cold metal bracelets on her wrists.

*　　*　　*

Todd arrived at the squad cars just as the police officers emerged from the tunnel leading the secret society members in handcuffs. It was all over. There was William White, Peter Wilbourne, and . . . Celine Boudreaux? Todd shook his head in disbelief.

Then he stopped breathing. His heart dropped. There was Elizabeth—enveloped in the arms of Tom Watts.

It's not too late, he told himself. *It's still not too late.*

Chapter
Ten

Steven put down the phone without saying a word and turned to Billie. All the blood had drained from his face.

"I can't take it," he gasped. "Being a brother is too hard." He took Billie by the arms. "Promise me we'll never have kids. If being a brother is this hard, being a parent must be a killer."

"What?" Billie cried. She led him to the couch and sat him down again. "What's wrong? What happened?"

"It was the police," Steven said.

Billie gulped and put her hand to her throat.

"Oh, it was nothing, really," Steven said blithely, waving his hand in the air. "Just that Elizabeth was kidnapped and almost killed, but saved at the last minute by an ex–football star."

Steven put his head in his hands. "Billie, I think I'm going to have a heart attack. I can't take it. The next thing I'll hear is that Mike got out of bed and walked to the bathroom by himself."

Just then the phone rang again.

"Oh no," Steven moaned, rolling over into the pillows.

Billie snatched the receiver. Steven watched her face as it changed from serious, to shocked, to disbelieving, to joyful.

"I understand, Jess," Billie said into the receiver. "Yes, of course . . . uh-huh, uh-huh . . . Of course, if he wants to see us . . . Thank you."

The second Billie put down the phone, she screamed. She jumped off the couch, pulled Steven to his feet, and hugged him as hard as she could.

"What's going on?" Steven demanded. "What's this all about? Everyone's going crazy!"

Billie doubled over, laughing uncontrollably. "I *have* lost my mind!" She kissed him on the lips.

"Don't tell me Mike walked," Steven said.

"No. Not quite that good."

"Well, what then?"

"Your arraignment hearing is going to be tomorrow."

Steven turned his palms to the ceiling. "What's so great about that?"

"Mike agreed to tell the judge what happened. He's going to tell him it was his fault, that he's not going to press charges. You are going to leave that courtroom a free man!"

Jessica was holding Mike's hand when he woke up.

He smiled weakly. "You've changed," he whispered. He reached up to touch her cheek, but his arm fell in exhaustion. "You look even more beautiful today than you ever did."

Jessica twisted in her chair. The last thing she wanted to hear right now was compliments.

"I had a dream," Mike said. "I had a dream that we got married all over again, this time a real wedding. A big church, a minister, a tuxedo and a wedding dress, the whole thing."

Jessica couldn't smile. How many times had she had the same dream? And how many times had that dream been shattered by Mike staggering drunkenly through the door?

"I'm weak," Mike said. "I'm jealous. I think every bad thing I did to you was driven by the fear that you'd leave me for another kind of life, that you were ashamed of me."

But Jessica was afraid—afraid of the decision she'd made. It had come to her like one of those big important truths of life. She had to stay with him.

Yes, she was just a college freshman, with all her life ahead of her. But for the first time ever, she was going to take responsibility for what she'd done. She had married Mike. She had promised to love him for better or worse. By marrying Mike she'd declared herself an adult, and she was going to act like one.

She'd been trying to reach Elizabeth for hours to ask her advice, but there'd been no answer at her dorm room. Jessica was by herself on this one. The final decision had to be hers alone. And it was. *That's how it should be,* she thought. She'd counted on Elizabeth to bail her out for too long now.

Jessica closed eyes, then opened them again.

"Mike," she said, tightening her grip on his hand. She cleared her throat. "I married you. I can't abandon you when times get bad."

Mike looked up at her, surprised. His eyes narrowed. "People shouldn't stay together out of obligation, only out of love," he said.

Jessica looked at him in amazement. He sounded so different. He was right. He *had* changed.

"I need you, Jess," he said. "And I love you. But it takes two people's love for a marriage to last. Jessica"—Mike reached for her hand and held it in both of his—"what I need to know is . . . do you *love* me?"

The question caught Jessica by surprise, like a bombshell. She wasn't sure why. It seemed like such a simple thing to figure out. Something she should certainly know. Except that everything—her entire life—relied on the answer.

"Do you love me, Jess?" Mike pleaded.

Jessica opened her mouth to reply but nothing came out. She closed it. *Don't I love him?* she asked herself. *Isn't that what I've been saying all along? If I do, why can't I just say, Yes, Mike, I love you and always will?*

Elizabeth watched over Tom's shoulder as William, Celine, Peter Wilbourne and the other secret society members were herded into a police truck. The truck pulled away, lights whirling and sirens blaring. Elizabeth clutched Tom around the waist and buried her face in his shoulder. She hadn't let go of him since the fight. She was afraid that if she did, she'd collapse. With her ear pressed against his beating heart, she could sense a bond between them so strong that it almost frightened her.

"Elizabeth, the police need me to come down to the station with them to make a statement," Tom said, pulling away gently.

She hadn't realized she'd been crying until he wiped a tear from her cheek. "Okay," she said, attempting a smile.

"I might have to stay until the arraignment hearing in the morning to make a statement. Why don't you go back to your room and try to get some sleep. I'll come find you there later?"

Elizabeth nodded. He tenderly pushed her hair back from her face and gave her a last long look before he turned away and climbed into a police car.

When the last of the cars had pulled away, she found herself standing alone in the bushes near the abandoned entrance to the tunnel at the back of the dark sprawling Sigma House. She could see the sky lightening, dawn coming like a pale smudge across the horizon. Her knees shook, her teeth chattered—not because it was cold but because every cell of her arms and legs was vibrating with strain and exhaustion and fear. Her brain knew the ordeal was over, but her body hadn't figured it out yet.

Relax, she told herself, peering into the dark around her. She started walking the half-mile or so to her dorm. She was still paranoid. She felt like every bush and tree was staring at her.

Then one of the trees moved. As a pale figure came toward her Elizabeth swallowed a shriek. She whirled and started running back across campus toward the dorms. She glanced over her shoulder. The figure was sprinting after her.

"No!" she cried upward into the night, trying to draw attention. "Stay away!"

He was catching up to her. He was so close she could hear his pounding footsteps closing in, his breathy panting. When she reached the middle of the quad, she felt fingers close around her elbow.

"No!" Elizabeth shrieked, tugging her elbow away. "Leave me alone!"

"Elizabeth, it's me!"

The voice sounded familiar, but Elizabeth was panicking. "Just leave me alone!"

"Liz, it's me. It's Todd!"

Elizabeth stopped and turned. Todd almost ran right into her. They faced each other in the middle of the grassy expanse.

"Todd, what are you doing here?" Elizabeth demanded, trying to catch her breath and calm her paranoia.

"I—I was scared. I wanted—" Todd dropped his gaze to the ground and tried to find the words he wanted.

"You won't believe what happened—" Elizabeth began, filling up the silence.

"I know," Todd said. "I saw everything."

He saw me with Tom? she wondered. She felt a momentary pang, as if she had done something wrong. The old instincts coming back.

"You saw everything?"

"I got there at the end, when you were all

209

coming out. The police cars. The guys in handcuffs . . ." Todd reached for Elizabeth and took one of her hands in both of his. "Liz, I don't care about Tom. I'm not jealous."

Elizabeth looked at him in surprise and confusion, unsure of what to say.

"I've been chasing you around campus all night," Todd went on. "I saw the news story, then I saw your door was knocked down and I knew something was wrong. I knew I had to save you, so I ran all over the place trying to find you."

"Todd—"

"I wanted to save you because I *needed* to," Todd continued in a rush. "Oh, Elizabeth, I'm so sorry for everything that happened between us."

Elizabeth could see the shimmer of tears in his eyes. He was gripping her hand so hard it hurt.

"I still love you. I always have," he said, his voice trembling.

"You have?" Elizabeth asked.

"I was an idiot and a jerk. I don't blame you for being angry at me. I treated you badly at the beginning of the semester. I was so full of myself I didn't even think about how you felt. That's all changed now. I've been through a lot."

"Todd, I—"

"Liz, I want to get back together. Forget

Lauren. Forget Tom. It's you and me. Like the old days. Like it always was. We were meant for each other. We always have been."

He looked around. "Remember this place?" he asked.

Elizabeth didn't have to look. She knew where they were standing. How many times had they walked through this place the first few days of college? All those stars she'd wished on. All those broken promises.

"Yes, I remember," she said bitterly.

"Please, Elizabeth," Todd said, squeezing her hand tighter. "What do you say?" His eyes were filled with the pale dawn light, glittering with anticipation.

"What do I say?" she echoed him. *What do I feel?* she asked herself.

She looked at Todd. It was like looking at a place she used to live—like when her family moved across town when she and Jessica were little. Whenever she saw the old house, she remembered all the good times. But it didn't make her want to live there again.

She liked where she was. She felt older, more powerful. The future seemed limitless. Todd's smile was a smile she remembered from moonlit walks and romantic evenings snuggled on the couch watching videos. His voice was so familiar, she knew she could recognize it in her sleep. But Todd looked like the past.

He said he wanted her back. Those were words she'd been hoping to hear for so long. All those tearful, lonely nights of missing him and wondering what had gone wrong.

He wanted her back, but did she want him? After everything he had done to her?

Looking up at Todd's face, Elizabeth felt sure she had loved him once. All these months, she now had to admit to herself, she'd secretly believed she still loved him, secretly hoped they could somehow go back to the time when they meant everything to each other. She hadn't been able to trust her heart to anyone else.

But standing in the new dawn light, she felt like she was hurtling forward away from her past into her future. Ahead of her loomed someone else, his arms outstretched to her. It was Tom. Tom who'd risked his life to save hers. Tom who made her heart pound and her knees weak. She knew where her heart belonged now.

Elizabeth pulled her hand away.

"I'm sorry, Todd," she said at last. "I loved you. Maybe some part of me always will. We grew up together. That will never change." She took a deep breath. "And I don't blame you for breaking up with me. It hurt really badly at the time, and I thought I'd never get over it. But finally I have, and I can see that it was good it happened."

"Elizabeth, no—"

She put her hand on Todd's cheek. "You gave us both a chance to be free and explore."

"So we did that!" Todd said in frustration. "We explored. We did other things, we met other people. Now it's time to be together again. We can be like we were before," he pleaded.

"No, we can't," Elizabeth said.

"Why? Don't you want to be that happy again?"

"I am happy, Todd."

Todd took a step back.

"Is it Watts?" he asked, his face twisting in pain. "Is it because you're in love with him?"

"He has something to do with it. But it's more than him. It's everything—" she said. "I can't explain it," she told him, shaking her head. "But I do know we can never go back. We have to move forward."

"Then we'll more forward together!" he begged.

"No," she said softly. "I can't."

Todd began to stalk away.

"Todd!" Elizabeth called after him. *That's not how I wanted to end it,* she thought to herself, watching him get smaller and smaller.

Before Todd reached the other end of the quad, he spun and called out. His voice bounced off the academic halls, the student union, the SVU chapel, spiraling up into the warm California morning.

"It's not over, Elizabeth!" he cried. "It'll never be over. I don't care what you say! I'm never going to let you go!"

Mike's question echoed off the blank walls in Jessica's mind: "Do you love me, Jess? Do you love me?"

Jessica started to move her mouth to answer. *Yes*, the voice in her mind answered. *Yes*. But she couldn't make her lips form the word. Why couldn't she just say it? Then it occurred to her. She knew her mind's answer, but what about her heart?

What's the point of lying anymore? she thought wearily. *I'm tired of all the lying.*

You could run away from responsibility. You could run away from school. You could even run away from your husband. But the one thing she could never escape was the truth: she wasn't ready to be married.

"I *do* love you, Mike. I really do—"

"But?"

"But—"

Mike loosened his grip on her hand and let it drop. "You should never have married me. You're too young. You have all your college years and your freedom ahead of you."

He took her hand again and held it stronger than ever.

"But I love you, Jess. And I want what's best for you, even if it means I can't have what I want." His eyes filled with tears. "I don't know why I was stupid enough to think it would work. I shouldn't have known it couldn't. As soon as I get out of here I'm going to have our marriage annulled."

Out of nowhere, a wind of relief blew through Jessica. She didn't know what to say. She hadn't known she'd been praying for Mike to release her with just those words.

Jessica leaned over and hugged Mike. She saw his tears spilling down his cheeks and reached up to wipe them away. But Mike caught her hand. Suddenly it struck Jessica: she couldn't be that for him ever again. She couldn't be the one to comfort and love him. Gaining her freedom meant losing Mike.

"Will I see you later at the hearing?" he asked.

"Mike," Jessica began. She looked away, embarrassed. "You talked to the D.A.? About Steven?"

"I'll call him now, Jess. Trust me."

"Do you want me there? At the hearing?"

"I do," he said.

Jessica turned before she started to cry. She

remembered the last time Mike had said "I do"—in the wedding chapel in Las Vegas. She'd never realized how those two words could be used at such different times in such different ways.

Jessica walked to the door of his room.

She looked back. His face was filled with such sadness it made her heart ache. *Go,* she ordered herself. *Take this chance and don't look back.* He was watching her go. Jessica smiled uncertainly, her own warm tears rolling down her face, and walked out the door.

As Jessica ran out of the hospital a storm of emotions swept her along, by the nurses at the nurses' station, past all the other patients toward the exit. The tears were falling, her breath was coming in ragged sobs. She wasn't happy, but she was free.

As she burst through the doors into the cool Southern California dawn, she felt a huge weight lift off· her shoulders. She felt light, lighter than ever. She was a new woman, and she knew how lucky she was to have a second chance.

She felt like running across the lush, sunlit campus as fast as she could.

Just a college girl, she reminded herself, *ready to start college—and life—all over again. And this time I'm going to do it right.*

*   *   *

Winston had Denise up against the wall of his dorm room. It was something he'd seen Clint do in one of the Dirty Harry movies. The girl came into the room, and before she said a word or even shut the door behind her, Clint had her pinned against the wall and was nibbling at her throat.

"Hey, now," Denise said, pushing Winston away.

Winston blinked at her.

"Oh, Winnie," Denise said. "You're so cute. I saw that movie, too."

"Then what's wrong? What did I do wrong?"

Denise breathed deeply. "Nothing," she said. "You got the move just right. I just needed to catch my breath."

She grabbed Winston by the collar and reeled him in like a fish. Winston backpedaled, and the two of them fell giggling onto his bed.

Then Winston was hovering above the bed, watching Denise and himself rolling back and forth below. He felt like an angel, separated from the earthly world.

I can't believe it, he said to himself. *Look at me down there. It's finally going to happen. After all these months, all these years. After this night no one will call me Winnie again. From now on it's Winston Egbert. Win, if you're lucky.*

217

Denise's silky hair was everywhere. Winston buried his nose in it and breathed. It smelled like rain.

The little brass buttons of her blouse were in his hands. One after the other they popped through their openings. First, an inch of Denise's delicious throat . . . then another . . . then another. It was like a dream.

This isn't so hard, he thought. *What's the big deal?*

Winston reached. Her skin was so soft, and warm, and . . . then he felt his fingers caught in a pinching vise.

"Ow!" he cried, pulling back his hand.

"Whoa there, big boy," Denise said, rolling off him. "What's the rush? We have three and a half more years! All things will come to he who waits."

"Case number two!" the bailiff announced. "The people versus Steven Wakefield."

The courtroom hummed with excitement. Steven's lawyer had told Jessica and Billie that if Mike kept his word, then all this would be a formality and Steven would walk out a completely free man.

The doors opened at the back and the courtroom grew quiet. Jessica didn't have to turn around to know why. She could hear the rubber wheels squealing across the polished wood floor. Two nurses accompanied Mike. One pushed his wheelchair while the other carried a bag of emergency equipment. As Mike passed her in his chair Jessica could feel his gaze on her. But she didn't look up until Mike had been rolled beside the district attorney at the prosecution's table.

She still felt terrible. Terrible that she was leaving him. And terrible that she knew now more than ever that it was the right thing to do.

"Come to order!" the bailiff called. "This court is now in session."

"Steven Wakefield," the judge said. "Stand before this bench."

Jessica saw Steven's lawyer look toward Mike as they stood up. But Mike didn't respond. She thought he looked more haggard than when she'd left him at the hospital. As if it weren't hours since she'd seen him but long, hard days of pain. His cheeks were sunken, his chin unshaven. He looked distracted, as though he had no idea where he was. His lips moved as if he was mumbling to himself. Jessica knew it meant trouble. This was the way Mike had looked when he came home drunk and started throwing things. When he was totally unpredictable. And capable of anything.

She looked up worriedly at Steven. He was

trying to get Mike's attention. He'd told her beforehand that he wanted to shake Mike's hand and call a truce.

"Steven Wakefield," the judge began. "You are charged with assault with a deadly weapon and attempted murder in the second degree. How do you plead?"

Steven looked confused. Billie half-stood and clenched Jessica's hand. Steven's lawyer tried to get the district attorney's attention, but the district attorney refused to look his way. He sat beside Mike, looking straight at the judge with a pleasant grin on his face.

"How do you plead?" the judge repeated, exasperated. "What is wrong with everyone today? Can nobody in this courtroom give me a straight answer?"

"But I thought—Mike said he would—" Steven stopped himself. Whispering swept through the spectators.

"Order!" the judge boomed. He turned toward Steven's lawyer. "What is your client talking about?"

"Your Honor," the lawyer said, "my client has been led to believe that these charges against him would be dropped."

The judge looked surprised. "On what grounds?"

"On the grounds that Michael McAllery confessed to owning the gun that was used to shoot him, and that the shooting was his fault, not my client's."

The courtroom erupted.

"Order!" The judge brought down his gavel with a crash. He directed his steely gaze at the spectators. "If you make any more noise I will have this courtroom cleared! Now then, Mr. District Attorney, maybe you can shed some light on this matter."

The district attorney rose. "I have nothing to say, Your Honor. Mr. McAllery made no such confession to me. You can see what kind of condition he is in. Clearly he would not have done this to himself. Steven Wakefield stands as charged."

Jessica jumped to her feet.

"Will you sit down, young lady?" the judge ordered.

But Jessica didn't. "Mike," she said. "You promised."

"Sit down!"

"Mike, you know it wasn't Steven's fault. You know this isn't about Steven. It's about me. Don't use Steven to get back at me!"

"Bailiff, have that young lady removed from the court!"

Two guards grabbed Jessica by the arms and began to lead her out.

"Mike, it's not going to change anything! Don't hurt Steven because of me. Please!" she shouted.

Jessica was nearly out the doors when the silent court echoed with the sound of Mike's voice. He tried to pry himself out of his wheelchair, then collapsed.

"Your Honor," he began weakly. "Don't let her go."

The judge held his hand up to his ear. "I'm sorry, son? What was that?"

"I said don't let them take her out," Mike said. It seemed to take all his strength to speak. He looked weaker and weaker. "She's right, Your Honor. I did promise her."

"You promised what, Mr. McAllery?"

"I promised her I'd tell the truth."

The judge glanced around the courtroom. He was beginning to look irritable. "And what *is* the truth? What exactly is going on here?"

Mike's answer was no more than a whisper. "It wasn't Steven Wakefield's fault."

Everyone in the courtroom froze. It was so quiet, Jessica could hear the window curtains rustling in the breeze.

"But he did shoot you, Mr. McAllery? You should be advised that even if it wasn't Mr. Wakefield's fault, if he did in fact pull that trigger, he could still be charged."

Jessica looked back and forth between Steven and Mike. As far as she knew Steven *had* pulled the trigger. But it was in self-defense. She was certain of that.

From where she was standing, she could see beads of sweat breaking out on her brother's forehead. Billie was holding her breath. All eyes were on Mike, who sat slumped in his wheelchair.

"Mr. McAllery, the court is waiting," the judge said.

Mike twisted around as far as he could and strained to take a last look at Jessica. He straightened in his chair and made himself as tall as he could.

"Your Honor, I came into Steven Wakefield's apartment looking for his sister. M-my wife. We were fighting. I didn't know what I was doing. Steven stepped between us to protect her. We fell to the ground. We fought. When he tried to get the gun away from me, I tried to shoot him. But I didn't shoot him."

Mike looked across the courtroom at Steven. "I shot myself instead."

The district attorney buried his face in his hands.

The courtroom erupted again.

The judge pounded his gavel and stood. "Case dismissed!"

The guards flanking Jessica let her go. She ran

223

down the aisle. Everyone was standing around Steven. Billie had thrown her arms around him. Others were pumping his hand. Jessica turned and saw Mike in his chair, sitting alone at the other end of the room.

She walked across the distance between them, bent down, and pressed her lips to his forehead. As they touched, and as she smelled the still-familiar smell of her husband, she knew she was touching him for the last time.

"Thank you," she whispered in his ear.

Mike looked up at her. He took her hands in his and squeezed them once. "Don't thank me, Jess. This is the way it was supposed to turn out."

As the nurse pulled him back he mouthed the words she had come to know so well: *I love you, Jess.*

Jessica watched tearfully as the nurses wheeled Mike through the courtroom doors and into the waiting ambulance.

She heard someone calling her name. She turned to her brother and Billie and their friends. It was as if she was seeing them for the first time. They all looked new to her. The light was clearer. Their laughter sharper.

Jessica knew what this feeling was.

It was the beginning of her new life.

*   *   *

The long, hot shower did Elizabeth some good. She'd let the steam build to a thick fog until she couldn't see her hands in front of her face. It was like floating in the clouds. She was too exhausted to think. The panicky flashes, the feeling of falling into a bottomless pit, vanished. The picture of Todd running away from her faded. She just let the warm steam wash over her and clean out her mind.

She toweled off slowly, then started walking back to her room. She hadn't realized how sore she was. Everything hurt—her neck, her knees.

When she stepped through the broken door, she drew in a sharp breath.

Tom was standing in the middle of her room. Suddenly her heart was pounding. She'd never been so happy to see anyone in her life. She wanted to run to him and embrace him, but she stopped herself.

"Oops," she said, grinning sheepishly. Above and below her towel were wide swaths of her bare golden skin. And underneath the towel . . . well, there wasn't much.

Tom was gazing at her with open admiration. Their eyes locked. She felt a blush warming her cheeks.

"I think I'll just put on something . . . um, less comfortable," Elizabeth said, snatching her blue jeans and a T-shirt.

"Don't do anything on my account!" Tom called after her. She could hear the laughter in his voice.

Elizabeth's mind was spinning as she walked into the bathroom and slipped on her Levi's and pulled a T-shirt over her head. She shook out her damp, fragrant hair and looked in the mirror.

The face caught her by surprise. It was a face she hadn't seen in a long time. Not since she'd left home and Sweet Valley High—the world in which she'd been a star. It was a confident, happy face, and she felt a surge of joy at seeing it again. It was the Elizabeth she'd known back home, but older, more grown up. She smiled at her reflection before she turned and walked out, letting the door of the bathroom close softly behind her.

Tom was standing by the window, looking out, with his hands thrust deep in his pockets. When he saw her he smiled.

Time seemed to pass slowly as she walked toward him, her gaze fixed on his heartbreakingly handsome face. For the first time in her life, she knew what true love was. She stepped silently toward him, unsure of what she was supposed to do, carried only by a pull in her heart.

Love wasn't holding on to the past, she realized, or hanging out with someone comfortable and affectionate, like Todd. It was the deep ache

226

in her throat and the tears of joy that were trying to come. It was a need so great that it felt
like pain. He held out his arms to her. She
folded herself in his embrace. Pressed against his
body she could feel the beating of his heart.

Tom. At last it's really Tom. The man she'd
fallen so helplessly in love with. The one she'd
dreamed about, wanted with all her heart.

She turned her face up to his, and he
kissed her. It was a breathless, weightless feeling. His lips on hers, soft then growing more
urgent. Her hands explored his broad muscular shoulders, crept up to his neck, his soft,
thick hair.

Their bodies wrapped together, they shuffled
blindly toward the bed and collapsed on it.
Their kisses grew so intense she felt she was
drowning in them. His strong hands searched
the curving lines of her waist, her back, her
long, silky hair.

"Elizabeth," he whispered as they drew
apart. "I've wanted this for so long." He kissed
her under her chin, down her neck to the base
of her throat. She felt a shiver travel the length
of her body. "I was too afraid to try." His voice
was so soft she barely heard him.

The poem. The beautiful poem that had made
her cry. "It was you," she whispered.

He pulled her into his arms again. "Of

course it was me." Her lips found his and she felt herself drown in another kiss.

Tom's head rested on Elizabeth's chest. Her golden hair tickled his ear, fell onto his shoulder. They lay there together, their clothes rumpled, their bodies intertwined after hours of kissing. The room was silent and still except for the afternoon sunlight moving across the floor.

He felt closer to her right then than he'd ever felt to anyone in his life. The force of his hunger for her, the feel of her body pressed to his took his breath away. There was so much pent up emotion after months of wanting her.

Now was the time to tell her a story he'd never told anyone. He wanted her to know. No more lies or misunderstandings. He needed her to know the truth.

Tom seemed to hear his voice before he'd decided exactly what he wanted to say.

"Two years ago everything changed for me," his voice was saying. "I was a different person then. Self-centered. Arrogant."

Elizabeth searched for his hand and laced her fingers through his.

"It was four or five games into the football season. Homecoming, the biggest game of the year was coming up. My parents had made it to a couple of games. We didn't have much money.

228

They couldn't afford to come every week. But I wanted my whole family there for that game."

Tom paused. His breath was even, his voice was calm. He had always been sure that the first time he told this story it would be impossible to get the words out. But here, in Elizabeth's arms, her heart beating a steady rhythm against his cheek, he knew he could.

"I told them they had to come, no matter what. I said that if they loved me, they'd come to the game. All of them, my parents, my older sister and little brother, everyone. They couldn't afford plane tickets, so they decided to drive. All the way from Colorado."

Tom took a deep breath. "At halftime, when I didn't see them in the seats I reserved for them, I went into the locker room, fuming. I was playing my best game ever. I'd passed for two touchdowns. Of all the games to miss, I thought. I threw things around. I kicked my locker. Then someone told me the news."

He looked up and his eyes met Elizabeth's. "The weather was terrible that weekend. Early snow in the mountains. There was . . . an accident."

He took a deep breath. "My whole family died that day. Everyone I loved. My older sister, who was a senior in college, my little brother, who was just starting high school. They had

229

their whole lives ahead of them. My parents, who'd sacrificed everything so I could go to college." There was a tremble in his voice. "My world ended that day."

Elizabeth held him tight. He saw tears fill her eyes.

"I felt like I killed them," he whispered.

"Oh, Tom," Elizabeth said softly.

He cleared his throat. "I told the coach that I wasn't finishing the game. I took off my pads and my helmet and dropped them at his feet. I quit right there."

He looked up at her and studied her lovely face for a long time.

"You know what I really wish, Elizabeth? I really wish they could have met you. You're everything my parents wanted for me."

Tom didn't realize he was crying until he saw a tear drop onto Elizabeth's T-shirt. She cradled his head as he cried, her tears mixing with his.

"I love you, Tom Watts," she whispered through her tears.

"I love you, Elizabeth Wakefield."

SIGN UP FOR THE SWEET VALLEY HIGH® FAN CLUB!

Hey, girls! Get all the gossip on Sweet Valley High's® most popular teenagers when you join our fantastic Fan Club! As a member, you'll get all of this really cool stuff:

- Membership Card with your own personal Fan Club ID number
- A Sweet Valley High® Secret Treasure Box
- Sweet Valley High® Stationery
- Official Fan Club Pencil (for secret note writing!)
- Three Bookmarks
- A "Members Only" Door Hanger

- Two Skeins of J. & P. Coats® Embroidery Floss with flower barrette instruction leaflet
- Two editions of *The Oracle* newsletter
- Plus exclusive Sweet Valley High® product offers, special savings, contests, and much more!

Be the first to find out what Jessica & Elizabeth Wakefield are up to by joining the Sweet Valley High® Fan Club for the one-year membership fee of only $6.25 each for U.S. residents, $8.25 for Canadian residents (U.S. currency). Includes shipping & handling.

Send a check or money order (do not send cash) made payable to "Sweet Valley High® Fan Club" along with this form to:

SWEET VALLEY HIGH® FAN CLUB, BOX 3919-B, SCHAUMBURG, IL 60168-3919

NAME _____
(Please print clearly)

ADDRESS _____

CITY _____ STATE _____ ZIP _____
(Required)

AGE _____ BIRTHDAY _____ / _____ / _____

Offer good while supplies last. Allow 6-8 weeks after check clearance for delivery. Addresses without ZIP codes cannot be honored. Offer good in USA & Canada only. Void where prohibited by law.
©1993 by Francine Pascal   LCI-1383-193

Life after high school gets even *Sweeter!*

Jessica and Elizabeth are now freshmen at Sweet Valley University, where the motto is: Welcome to college — welcome to freedom!

Don't miss any of the books in this fabulous new series.

♥ College Girls #1	0-553-56308-4	$3.50/$4.50 Can.
♥ Love, Lies and Jessica Wakefield #2	0-553-56306-8	$3.50/$4.50 Can.
♥ What Your Parents Don't Know #3	0-553-56307-6	$3.50/$4.50 Can.
♥ Anything for Love #4	0-553-56311-4	$3.50/$4.50 Can.
♥ A Married Woman #5	0-553-56309-2	$3.50/$4.50 Can.
♥ The Love of Her Life #6	0-553-56310-6	$3.50/$4.50 Can.

Bantam Doubleday Dell
Books for Young Readers

Bantam Doubleday Dell
Dept. SVU 12
2451 South Wolf Road
Des Plaines, IL 60018

Please send the items I have checked above. I am enclosing $_____ (please add $2.50 to cover postage and handling). Send check or money order, no cash or C.O.D.s please.

Name _____

Address _____

City _____ State _____ Zip _____

Please allow four to six weeks for delivery.
Prices and availability subject to change without notice.   **SVU 12 4/94**